THE VICTORIA CHRONICLES VOLUME II

Godwin OJI

INVICTOR BOOKS

ISBN: 9798746065995

Cover design by: Art Painter
Library of Congress Control Number: 2018675309
Printed in the United States of America

*To all who have Lived and Laughed and Loved in Old Victoria, and
to those who haven't.*

*And I dare not forget those who have contributed in one way or
the other, to making this volume reality, I say thank you.*

*A special thank you reading it now, and to the dimpled one for
the wonderful reviews, and to all those who have contributed
to making Victoria the wonderful magical place that it is.*

PROLOGUE

Down, the stream
Down the stream canoes laid down
When the fishermen are sleeping
Sweet sons of earth are dreaming
Down the coastal town of Victoria, down the stream

SCHOLA'S GHOST

The ghost of the young woman everybody would come to know as Schola, first appeared in the Botanic Gardens on the first day of January 1961. She appeared to three fishermen who were very, very drunk at the time, after consuming a fair amount of Afofo. It was the morning after the New Year's eve.

On account of the state of intoxication of the three fishermen, a fair section of Victoria's inhabitants did not take the report seriously. Those who did, assumed she would go away, as many other ghosts had done before her.

But Schola did not go away. She reappeared every day of that fateful January, to a teacher, a bricklayer and a good number of distinguished citizens of Victoria.

The apparitions were always on the same path, between the Miramar Hotel and the Zoo. The Ghost sightings were so frequent, talk of them replaced the normal arguments as to whether Powercam Football club, was a better team than the Public Works football club.

They could have carried on talking about Schola without doing very much about her, but for a most peculiar apparition.

One day, Schola appeared separately to the lovers of the sitting chairman of the Victoria Native Authority Council; his two girl-friends, Eposi and Effeti, and his one wife, Limunga. At this point, the inhabitants of Victoria agreed, the time had come for action.

They resolved to bring in Manyaka.

Manyaka was the most famous witch doctor in Muyuka, a hot and humid cassava town to the south of Kumba. He collected seven white pigs from the Native Authority heads of the town's seven main quarters, as recompense for his future magical services. But the people in the quarter of Gardens were taxed extra.

This extra tax logic, was so logical, even the good people of Gardens acquiesced to it without much protest. The reasoning was, since the ghost made her apparitions in the Botanic Gardens from which the quarter of Gardens got its name, Gardens therefore, had a greater responsibility for the ghost.

The quarter gave, in addition to a pig, a crate of rather strong German Schnapps. Luckily for them, they did not have to go to Germany for it. They had Country Man Spirits and Beer whole-sale distributors nearby in Church Street, just after the Ngokika bridge. (Manyaka had explicitly asked for German Schnapps, the one with the red key on the bottle).

But all was not plain sailing. Negotiations for the payment for Manyaka's efforts, briefly reignited an old quarrel. This quarrel was on the thorny question of whether certain town sections, were indeed quarters in their own right. For example, was Cow fence, Clerk quarters, and GRA, quarters, or sections of Down beach and Bota. This was settled in the usual manner. They agreed to discuss it during the next democratic parliamentary elections.

The powerful witch doctor arrived in Victoria to great fanfare. He shouted incantations, cast spells, and banished Schola's ghost to wherever ghosts of young women went, when the living got tired of them. For the next ten days after his visit, nobody reported any sighting of Schola.

Then, on the eleventh day of March 1961, she appeared to three pupils of the Native Authority School in Bota Victoria. The pupils had gone to harvest Koolooba near the Miramar Hotel, during hours when they should have been learning a thing or two in class. Instead, they had played truant, and learnt that Schola's ghost did not harm little children like them.

Schola's refusal to go where the witch doctor had indicated, teased out the creative juices in the pupils of the Native Authority School Bota. They composed a song. It went;

"Schola, where did you come from? And Schola responded, by the way.

The next line went,

"Manyaka ele eli lelelele, by the way".

The song had a catchy tune, and held some clue about what the pupils thought of the witch doctor Manyaka.

Schola's defiance of Manyaka, the powerful, was a first. Manyaka's fame radiated from Muyuka, where he lived, and reached the Kupe hills deep in the humid forests to the North. People feared his amulets, charms, and ability to transform humans into animals.

Schola's reappearance, thus forced to the surface, a never hitherto entertained doubt. This doubt was the small question of the limits to Manyaka's powers. What if, what if he was not as powerful a witch doctor as they had believed?

They chewed on this thought for some long that some of the residents of Victoria were very much minded to march to Muyuka, and demand a refund of the pigs and the crate of very strong German Schnapps. But the stories of his erstwhile magical exploits, of turning people who crossed him into lizards, advised against this course of action.

The chief of Bota, Ekone Eyole, a good Christian by all accounts, and a firm believer in Manyaka, explained the re-apparition. He intimated, Schola had so appeared, because the Native Authority

School children Bota, were not Christians in good standing with the Lord. The ghost's apparition was testament to their deep heathen nature.

He was a resourceful man, quick on his feet with ideas. He went further, and pronounced that a white missionary in the service of the Most-High Jehovah, had indeed founded the town of Victoria, and based on this intelligence, he tabled they should resolve to use the power of Jehovah, to chase out poor Schola's ghost.

This Jehovah power, the chief further attested, was definitely more infinite than that of any witch doctor, irrespective of where the witch doctor resided. You see, back in the day, witch doctor power was dependent on their abode. At the bottom of the ladder was Muea, then Motombolombo, Muyuka, and at the top, you had Oku.

The chief of Mbonjo, added his mouth to this rather fine reasoning.

The townspeople could not fault the thinking of the two chiefs, and resolved to get a man of God to intervene, to prevent Schola from being the most talked about, and the most feared person in Victoria, dead or alive.

This decision to seek Divine intervention raised a new difficulty. Which of the earthly divine servants of the Most-High Jehovah to approach with the request?

Amongst the Presbyterians, the Baptists, and the Moslems in Liengu Mbokwe, there was not a tradition of binding spirits, and instructing them to leave the inhabitants of Victoria to their earthly paradise. The Pentecostals and the Holy Ghost fire people, were yet to establish footholds in the town. They were still busy bamboozling the people of Bamenda and Kumbo, up in the Grass fields to the north west of the country.

So, the good people of Victoria reasoned, that left only the Catholics. They alone had the knowledge, experience and skills, to perform the task at which the witch doctor Manyaka had proved woefully ineffectual.

The Native Authority, approached Father Mulligan, the respected Catholic man of God of the Holy Family Parish Newtown. They sang the song to him, the chart topping song the school children of the Native Authority School Bota, had composed.

-Schola, where do you come from? By the way.

When they finished singing, Father Mulligan insisted they told him what they knew of Schola. He said, this was to determine what section of the Holy Roman Catholic book of exorcism to use. The truth was, he did not believe the story proffered. He could not accept Schola had appeared from nowhere, from "by the way", as per the song.

Good old Father Mulligan conducted further Catholic investigations. He determined, Schola was indeed a young girl of thirteen or so, who had been raped and murdered.

He also learned the murder took place on that stretch of road in the Botanic gardens, between the Victoria Zoo and the Miramar hotel. She had been on her way to Big Mop market in Cassava farms, to sell cocoyams.

Father Mulligan located the necessary section for the exorcism of a town ghost, and, after much ecclesiastical research, he also located the subsection for a ghost, whose body had died of the foul crime of rape and murder.

The good priest also added to his exorcism manual, the verses of the New Testament where Jesus fed the hungry five thousand. This was because, Schola was engaged in the business of feeding the good people of Victoria. It was this good deed of feeding the hungry, that made it possible for some evil resident to carry out the foul and despicable act.

Father Mulligan chose a Sunday for the exorcism. The Native Authority showed their authority on temporal matters and declared the Sunday so chosen, a public holiday. The Priest then set about choosing seven priests experienced in casting out ghosts.

On the appointed Sunday, which was the last Sunday of April 1961, the good priests dressed up in fine red and white flowing robes. They donned impressive pointed hats, and the town's people gathered on the path where Schola had been sighted over, and over again. They sang hymns interspersed with readings from the Catholic prayer of contrition.

As they sang, the seven priests moved about their incense carriers. They drenched the path on which Schola had appeared with gallons of holy water. By the time they finished, there was so much water on the path, a visitor to that section of town, would have assumed the river Limbe had overflowed its banks.

That evening, after the drowning of the path with Holy water, the good people of Victoria held a small 'eat and drink' in the Centenary stadium.

But the next week, Schola ignored the Catholic Father Mulligan. She reappeared to five children from the Our Lady of Lourdes Catholic primary school in Gardens, who were rather fine Christians.

This brought into question, the chief of Bota's earlier pronouncements on the spirituality of the good children of the Native Authority School Bota. It also cast some doubt on the efficacy of Jehovah, as worshipped by the Catholics.

A religious war nearly ensued. Chief Moomba of the native authority of Liengu Mbokwe dispersed the gathering dark religious war clouds, by suggesting, maybe, this was a matter for the police.

But the police then, were as ineffectual as they are today.

The police representative on the Native Authority board questioned whether it was workable to arrest a ghost, and lock it up in the charge office. He respectfully declined to offer expert police services. That was the end of that.

Or so it might have appeared.

Meanwhile, the Schola song, the first-ever dance song composed in Bota, spread to other primary schools in old Victoria.

It became so ubiquitous, the Modeka Land and Investments Fortune's heiress, grew alarmed. She owned a pop band, the Victoria Nightingales, and she had her sights set on the group coming out with a Christmas number one. So, she intervened to stop the Schola song from topping the school playground charts, and tabled a proposal that, the only solution to the apparitions, was a punishment to her murderer.

She preached the logic of this punishment, and faced quite an opposition on account of her womanhood. In the end, she impressed Mola Njoh with her eloquence. That was no mean achievement, given as Mola Njoh, was the most rabid chauvinistic misogynist in Victoria.

So that was how it came about that the people agreed, the rape and murder of Schola, had gone unpunished for too long. The heiress's proposal accumulated enough voices in support.

Back in the day, before the advent of vigilante groups, the police were the only people who could mete out punishment. The good people then went again to the head of the Victoria Police Constabulary and tabled accordingly.

The police opened a case this time, which, as the Modeka heiress mentioned, they should have done on the day of the murder.

With the case reopened, the police, as was their custom, proceeded to make various accusations and arrests. They arrested so many people; if the Native Authority chairman had not intervened, they would have arrested the entire male population of Victoria. They would have arrested them all, including the heads of the Native Authority.

The mass arrests stopped, and the sightings of Schola continued.

The police investigators then went deep undercover. In one of the many meetings the townsfolk had with the police, somebody mentioned something that would make the Chief inspector close the case.

She pointed out the police station, was only three hundred meters from the spot where Schola had been murdered.

So, it came to pass the case has since remained closed.

All because, of three hundred meters.

To this day, the people of Victoria report sightings of poor Schola's ghost. They see her during certain hours of the day in the Botanic Gardens, and Schola remains a scar on the conscience of the people of this God's own town, who would still rather she went away.

But some have now come to accept Schola's ghost is as much a part of the town of Victoria, as Alfred Saker, even though only Alfred Saker has a statue opposite the Victoria club in Down Beach.

Nonetheless, in Victoria, even today, the eyes of fair-minded citizens go moist, whenever the poor girl's name is mentioned.

A good number of them of any religious persuasion, still nurse the hope, one day, a statue will be erected in her honour.

A monument to remind the good people of Victoria, that men are capable of much evil, if they put their minds to it.

THE RISE AND RISE OF BOBBI-LONG-GO

Bobbi Long-Go was one of the boys the old men in the village of Karata on the border of Victoria to the west, had marked out for a life of quiet inconsequence. But, Bobbi was to prove them wrong.

True, the fire of the mountains behind his village, did not stir his blood. No huge passions fired his imagination, and his actions inserted no mirthful chapters into village history.

He did not join the boys who roamed the farms perched like bats on the mountainside, and left behind broken branches. Bobbi did not join the rude lads who squashed freshly dug mounds of cocoyam, as if an elephant high on palm wine, had performed a moonlight dance.

His father was a taciturn man, who, after his wife died in a freak accident that involved a guava tree, a hurricane lamp and some raw cocoyams, passed seamlessly from married life, to bachelorhood, and lived the rest of his life without much incident, and died, a happy man.

Bobbi Long-Go became, on more than one occasion, the fall guy for some impertinent act the other boys had committed. That is how he was to carry, on his back and buttocks, the punishment for the disappearance of Chief Motombi's goat.

The clever old men of the traditional council, refused to believe his confessed responsibility for the disappeared goat. But the steadfastness with which he stuck to the story, would have amazed even his own mother in her grave.

So it came to pass, that Bobbi Long-Go's punishment was dished out as a half-hearted thrashing in the village square, as if the disappearing of a goat, was a tolerable crime. The masquerade chosen to wield the whip of retribution, found his whipping arm slowing, because he knew Bobbi Long-Go was taking the rap for some obscure reward.

But the one thing Bobbi had in spades, and which the other boys, smarter, sharper, nonetheless lacked, was his ability to stick to a thing. When he had a task to perform, no matter how pedestrian, how absurd, he stuck to it like a grasshopper to the sap of a gum tree. Nowhere was this most vivid, as in what passed for his village school performance.

He passed his school days, munching pencil ends, and cracking biro bottoms, absentmindedly pulling out his hair. It took him ten years to complete the six years of study needed for the standard-six exams. But he got there in the end, even though the effort rendered him as bald as a China woman's bottom. Not that Bobbi knew any China women.

He eventually got a job, as the personal secretary to the chief of Service for Education for Fako Division, at the offices down the beach in old Victoria.

It was a great mystery to his friends and enemies alike, why he got the job. Some said, his wife was the Chief of Service for Education's mistress. This was understandable, given his wife was a rather pretty Batoke girl of tepid character, whom he had married on the strength of his standard six certificate. Some said it was because the service head only wanted somebody to run errands.

Whatever the reason, Bobbi Long-Go could be seen working late into the night, to complete some task or the other for his boss. When people saw the office bulbs burning into the wee hours of the morning, it transformed their suspicion that his boss had the first right of refusal on his wife, into certain knowledge.

It so happened that one day, Bobbi Long-Go was so engaged in completing a task, that he did not hear a car drive up to his office front. He only raised his head, when a rather bulky man opened the door to his office. Bobbi Long-Go stared at this man, his brain slowly grinding away from the task he was performing.

-Where's your boss? The man asked.

-He's gone home. It's late.

The man walked around the table, and stood behind Bobbi Long-Go. Bobbi swivelled in his chair to face him. That swivelling was the only act of defiance he had ever carried out in his life, and he soon regretted it, when he noticed the cut of the man's clothes.

-What're you doing?

-A report, sir.

-Why so late in the day?

-My boss asked me. It's urgent, and my boss's boss wants the report on Monday, and I've been at it for three weeks.

-Very well then, don't let me disturb you.

And with that, the man left.

Bobbi Long-Go scratched his head and returned to his work.

That Monday, the report was dispatched minchi minchi to Bobbi's boss's boss. Life carried on for Bobbi Longo-Go as per usual the next year. He passed his time running errands for his boss, working late, and looking after his wife, who had the singular luck, of bringing his first child into the world.

His wife will go on to have two sons and three daughters in cadence. They were fine children, and notwithstanding the fact that some evil chins pointed in the direction of his various bosses, is children will remain loyal to him.

Life could have carried on like tick-tock, tick-ticking tock, until the annual cycle of sending reports to Bobbi's boss's boss came around again.

Bobbi Long-Go was engaged in doing what he does best, burning free electricity at the office, when the same man as the last time, appeared.

-Have seen you somewhere. Bobbi said, as soon as the door opened, and he raised his head from his task.

-Am I that easy to forget? The man barked, and Bobbi's memory crackled into life.

He got up abruptly, remembered with shame, that he had been too shocked to stand the last time this man was here. He stood up so awkwardly, that his lap knocked over his table and the back of his knees, knocked over his chair.

-Sit down, sit down.

When Bobbi eventually up righted his table and chair, gathered the papers from the floor, the man said.

-Do you know who I am?

-No, sir.

-You're a Karata man, are you not?"

-Yes, sir.

-Good good. I can tell you this. You better start looking for an assistant.

Bobbi Long-Go did not know what to make of this. But before the sun could fire his bald pate six more weeks, what happened was Bobbi Long-Go's boss was suddenly transferred to some mosquito-infested part of the country, and Bobbi Long-Go was made Chief of Service.

Shock waves rippled through the town of Victoria. The town folks paid for dedicated Church services to attract Bobbi's kind of luck. Visits to witch-doctors multiplied with the same requests. They could not think of any other reason for Bobbi Long-Go's good fortune.

Bobbi set about finding an assistant. He thought long and hard. In the end, he realised that the only way he would really really enjoy this his newfound power, was to promote somebody like him, to his former job.

He did find somebody like him Mr Ngombe, and got the same service as he had meted out to his erstwhile boss.

Then he got promoted from the provinces to the Capital, this time in charge of a whole ministerial department, and he did the same. He filled the corridors of the ministry with people like him, and the people like him did the same down the line.

In no time, the Ministry of Education and the entire civil service, was staffed with people after Bobbi Long-Go's own heart.

In the end, Bobbi Long-Go, the man from Victoria, became a very, very high functionary in the government of the country. And what was more, to him at least, he had the medals to show for it.

He grew fat, but not more than the others of his station, and like the others, he knew how to kiss arses bigger than his. He was not too corrupt, not too greedy, and only matched, the current corruption and greed barometer.

Bobbi-Long-Go lived to a fine old age, had many children and mistresses as befitting a man of his station.

He died eventually, like all good people did, but what he left behind has stood the test of time.

True, he was soon forgotten, though his children, either from his genes or their mother's, or the genes of the various bosses Bobbi Longo-Go had during his meteoric rise, fought hard and long to remember him. But even then, he eluded them.

The genius of Bobbi Long-Go thwarted them in the absence within it, of anything worth pointing as to the why of it, anything resembling a lasting legacy. He did not pass any new laws, build any new schools, nor induced anybody to think beyond the obvious. He drafted no new policies, and did not change the pictures on his office walls.

But still, he was a genius.

Bobbi Long-Go's genius was in keeping the graph of his country's progress, flat. His genius was in, when people looked back and wondered why their country, their continent, was in such a sorry state, and why such asinine people populated the higher ranks of the civil service, no one, not even the smartest amongst them, could trace the phenomenon, back to Bobbi-Long-Go.

And it is a good thing they could not, because it was no fault of Bobbi Long-Go's.

In the end, Bobbi-Long-Go had one lasting achievement. He thwarted the old men of his village, and those who have come after him, now know not to listen to old men, who never went anywhere beyond the confines of a village in the mountains high above Victoria.

WHY RICH MEN
HAVE NO FRIENDS.

Luck has always looked down on Ekinde, the way an Hausa man looks on swine meat. But still today, after waking up at five in the morning, he prays for luck, and leaves his house in Ngeme to visit his debtors.

He starts in Sokolo where he is unlucky. From there, he takes the road down through the CDC head office into GRA, where he collects from one Lefon, who works in the accounts department of the CDC. Then he goes past middle farms, down to Gardens, Mbenday, and then up to mile one. From Mile one, he catches a taxi to New Town.

In New Town, he is lucky, and he finds his oldest debtor Mbela, who was just about to go out.

The gods are smiling.

He gets back ten per cent of what he had set out to collect, and all that walking and asking, has made him very thirsty. For the millionth time that day, he wonders why he extends soft loans to people who did not have the decency to pay back.

The truth was, he is a generous, peace loving man. Try as much as he could; he could not refuse to share his money and his beer.

Nonetheless, he resolves he will never give out anything again, beer or money. He adds beer, because, in old Victoria, beer was more important than money. In fact, a man you give free beer, would love you more than a man you lend money on zero interest.

Now, it is three in the afternoon, and the sun is giving the town of Victoria the what-for, before it finally dies in amber swirls to the West coast.

Ekinde is taking what he calls, a cool-down, on a knocked together bench on the concreted veranda of Namondo's Off licence. He pours the contents of a cold bottle of Beaufort, into a tall glass, examines its colour at eye level, and tilts the glass into his half-opened mouth.

Then he savours the slide of amber liquid down his throat, and ignores the smell of last night's urine wafting up from the gutters. Ekinde is so engaged, when he sees a body walking upright, and looking left and right, on a sun-drenched Church Street.

The body is approaching the general direction of where he is sat, hidden by a tower of beer crates.

The body Ekinde notices walking upright and looking left and right, is not exactly making a bullet path towards him. But he knows if he does not act, there might be a change of direction in the body's movements, and then, he will be in line with the bullet. Being so in line, is not a proposition Ekinde particularly cares for at this moment. He does not, because the body walks with a clickety gait, and has the same vulture neck, as his long-time friend, Awoof Amos.

Now, if there is anybody Ekinde does not want to see at this point in the proceedings of his cooling down, it is the body of Awoof Amos.

He sighs. Things were going swimmingly until this moment.

Ekinde ducks low, crouches over his still cold bottle, knocks it over, drops his glass to the ground in an attempt to catch the bottle, and loses both.

He curses Awoof Amos aloud for the accident.

-Damn you, Awoof Amos.

And it is precisely this curse that Amos hears, or pretends to hear.

Amos's body movements come to a complete stop. His head swivels, and his mouth utters the most honest shout of surprise, at finding his best friend, Ekinde. He emits a second shout, because Ekinde was engaged in a cooling down all by himself, without the decency, of inviting Amos. Further, Awoof Amos considers this the utmost betrayal, as Ekinde was, and is fully aware, of his temporary financial difficulties, and the nefarious effects the dry-season sun has on his throat.

Amos comes short of calling his best friend, a monkey who eats alone, even though he thinks about it. But, to be fair, Ekinde has as good a reason as any would ever have, to be so crouching and spilling his cooling down beer.

The first reason is, in all cooling down sessions the two loving friends have had in the last ten years, the bill had fallen on Ekinde, and ten years is the length of time for which Amos's temporary financial difficulties, have lasted.

Added to that, the balance of loans between them stands at a level which, if Awoof Amos were to pay back the sums so borrowed, Ekinde would buy himself a small Nissan. Add if you add to that, the fact that Awoof Amos was gainfully employed at the ministry of town planning, you would understand why Ekinde was not so happy, at seeing his friend.

Amos installs himself on the bench next to his main man, and shouts to Namondo sitting behind the bar, fly-posted with brown and yellow '33 export' beer posters. He instructs her to add the cost of the beer coming his way, on the bill on which the beer Ekinde had been so engaged with, was found.

And as good friends do in Victoria, the damage to purse being firmly settled on one of them, they chat, laugh, and drink. They are on their third bottle each, when a young man steps onto the Namondo Veranda with an instant offer of riches.

Lottery scratch cards at a hundred francs each.

Now, Ekinde does not suffer fools gladly, more so, when his tongue and purse have been loosened, and he makes this known to the lottery ticket vendor.

-If the tickets were such a dead cert, as you announce, why don't you buy yourself one?

-I don't have the money; the lottery seller sighs with his eyes on Ekinde's rather sweaty bottle.

Now, Ekinde knows a lot of things. And he knows them better than he knows which bar to engage in cooling down, so that his loving friend Awoof Amos, would not find him.

-Well, I'll tell you this for free.

-Tell me what for free?

-You could borrow money from your sales, buy the scratch card, and when you win, since it is such a dead cert, you can reimburse your employer.

Ekinde leans his head back with a gratified air. He was happy to observe that his logic had got the lottery ticket seller scratching his head.

But Amos's new words shatter his peace.

- Ekinde, my brother, lend me a hundred francs, and I'll reimburse you. I swear.

People have always wondered how Awoof Amos secures his loans. It was easy. He goes straight for it, asks for it.

Ekinde has heard many stupid things in his time, but this one took all the bananas in Bonadikombo.

He stares at his friend in disbelief.

-So, you think you'll win?

Amos has never been surer, of anything in his life. He even had an itch in the centre of his palm, a sign he will touch some money before ere long.

-If you do not win, you pay me back with interest?

Now, Amos had never in his life, refused to pay interest; he just never paid the interest, and the loan's principal.

The first one hundred francs nearly won a million. This near million induces Ekinde to advance another hundred francs, without any prompt from Amos. Amos's scratching arm begins to hurt from scratching too many lottery cards. He says this was partly because of the beer, and partly because of the blazing sun.

But just about when Ekinde starts wondering whether he can settle the bill accumulated with Namondo, and Namondo too, starts to ask herself whether she should ask for a front up payment like the lottery seller is doing, Amos lets out an almighty whoopee.

-I have won!! Yes!!

-You sure?

They examine the amount revealed under the scratch panel of the blue and white card, and there is no mistaking the amount of 10,000,000 CFA.

Now, the two friends were never given to hugging and dancing. But this is exactly what they are doing, and a small crowd gathers on account of the excellence of their waltz. Even the lottery ticket vendor joins in.

The watchers start to clap, and Ekinde feels embarrassed. He let's go of Amos's waist, and the crowd disperses.

When they regain their seats, Amos asks Namondo for another round of beers, and says to his best friend.

-Well, well, my friend. Now, I can reimburse the two hundred thousand I owe you and the other loans outstanding.

Ekinde looks at Amos, and a fly whizzes close to his open mouth.

-But, it is my money that won the ten million.

Awoof Amos hitches up his trousers.

-My great friend and brother, you lent it to me, and I am offering to pay it back. Here, here, do take your money. All in all, it is ten thousand francs.

-So you had money all along, and borrowed mine to buy the tickets?

-Does it matter?

-Yes, by the way, it was not the hundred francs I lent you that won the ten million.

-But I was the one doing the scratching.

-Excuse me?

It is the lottery ticket seller.

-But you can share it, and maybe a little for me. It's a lot of money.

Amos finishes his beer, and gets up to leave with the Lottery ticket in his back pocket, and that is when Ekinde discovers he has the Mike Tyson uppercut. He goes low, into a deep stance, rises, pushes his thighs upwards, and presents Amos with a deadly right. Amos crumbles against the crates, his eyes roll to the back of his head.

Ekinde puts his hands in Amos's pockets for the lottery ticket, finds it, and transfers it to his own pocket.

THE NEW GIRL.

Amongst the pleasure girls who hung around the Miramar and the Makaya snack bars, it was considered a necessary skill, to be able to spot a recently arrived tourist. Failure to do so was bad for business.

And it was easy. The newbies stood out. They had pale skin, strange smells, and foreign condoms. They invariably drank whisky for two straight nights, and pretended they did not see us. We knew what they wanted, and they knew what we were looking for. But they still needed the two days of whiskey courage, before they asked for one of the girls. If the girl pushed back, played hard to get, they ran away with their money. If you were unlucky, you lost their custom forever.

You had to give them time, and after the two-night initiation, they pinched your bottom, and asked if your Wonderbra enhanced boobs, were natural. To which you replied,

-It'll cost you to find out.

And they paid handsomely if you scored, and you made more from that early encounter, than you would for the entire three or so months they hung around. Time which they used to understand the value of local money, time for their skin colour change, and time for their skin smell change.

In the same way we girls could tell the new tourists, so the regular customers could tell the new girls. But it was not because of their skin or its smell. Well, the smell came into the telling a little. New girls needed time. Time to accumulate foreign perfumes, punters brought back from holidays taken with wives and regular girlfriends.

I knew all the girls, including the part-time ones who travelled down from somewhere up- country, to see a cousin, and ended up working the odd two weeks. Time to amass a few shishis, before disappearing to whatever part of the country from out of which they had crawled. But I could go one farther and tell, not only a new girl, but also one who was new to the business.

I knew this girl was new straight away. She gave herself away because she ignored the business rule that, a new girl must spend her first night at a cousin's table.

I had come early. Business had been slow the previous night. All evening, I did not smell a single drink from a prospective client. This Saturday, as I watched the night crowd fill up the streets, I prayed. The women who sold roast fish and the men who sold pork, had set up their smoky charcoal stands. That was usually the sign that the evening was about to take off.

She walked into Makaya with a too big handbag, and a too blood-red silk blouse, cut high on the arm to show her beautiful arms.

-She's going to be bad for business all right, I said to myself.

The regulars loved the new girls, and we hated them, but I have been here long enough to know how to turn a new girl into an advantage. When a new hot girl turned up, you made sure she became your cousin, and sat at your table. That way, you picked up her leftovers.

She sat alone, a frail thing of a girl with long legs, big almond eyes, and the wrong clothes. You see, short skirts were compulsory, the clients who paid well, especially the French, loved them.

But here comes this little missus wearing grey flannel trousers and a blood-red blouse, as if she were going to a wedding down the mayor's office. She sat in a dark corner and even raised her glass to the neon lights on the ceiling, and shook her head.

When I got tired of watching her, I got up and danced next to the table where Big Joe usually sat. It was not yet nine, which was his arrival time.

The king of the regulars was Big Joe. He was a large man, Italian or French, who had stayed in Victoria for so long that, nobody bothered anymore whether he was from anywhere. He paid well, wore a wedding ring. On nights when he was not looking for adventure, he walked in, announced his evening chastity and shared his bottle of whisky, like a gentleman, unlike the customers who came in, bought you drinks, and you only realised that would be all you were getting, when it was too late to bag another client.

I tired of dancing in Big Joe's corner, walked over and said,

-Hey, cousin.

She raised her little head, and smiled. It was a broad smile. But her eyes did not smile. There was a look in them, like she was a hunter and was the hunted, at the same time.

I had seen that look once before. I tried to recall where, and failed.

-You want to join my table?

She smiled that smile again.

-Maybe, later.

I carried on gyrating in my corner, and watched the punters amble in, and kept an eye on those who arrived in groups. On the forecourt of Makaya, you learned that groups of more than three, spelt trouble. They drank too much, got too drunk, and were too broke by the end of the evening, to pay for your time. That is if they did not slip something in your drink.

Smart girls went for the lone customer. He had business on his mind, drank the right amount, and got straight to business.

A group of four tourists walked in, looked around the bar, checked my arse, and made for her table.

That was when I remembered where I had seen that look in her eyes.

That same look had been in my mother's eyes, the hour before she gave my father the what's what. I watched, with my heart in my mouth, as she waved her hand around the table, and the men sat down and shook her hand. I calmed the urge to rush to her, to give some advice from an old hand.

I have seen many a girl come here, sit down with three men, get roaring drunk and then disappear into the night. The next day, if they came back, they had long stories to tell. One girl, her name was Martha or Maggie, could not tell any stories the next day. We found her body three months later, washed up by the sea near the catholic church in Bota.

I carried on dancing until I could no longer contain the urge to protect this girl. I saw the waiter, Simon, carry over two bottles of champagne to her table, and made my move.

-Cousin, mind if I sit?

I thrust my hand in the men's faces in turn, and asked Simon for a chair and a champagne glass.

My Cousin smiled. She whispered in my ear.

-You're bold, Cousin. You like Champagne?

I smile back and sat. One of the men moved away from her to make space. It was not like I had not had champagne for a while. Big Joe bought one every now and then, and if you were around, you got a lucky glass.

The men only relaxed after the first bottle. I followed her into the toilets before they poured out the second.

-What's your name?

She smiled, the smile that had bothered me earlier. She said it would be better for me, if I did not know.

-You know; you remind me of my mother.

-I hope I don't look that old.

-No, not at all, you are very beautiful.

She laughed as she washed her hands.

-I hope you do not like girls, because I am not that way.

-No, no, I said.

I had forgotten about that.

-Just think of me as your cousin. Call me, No Name.

She spoke little, the men told dirty jokes, and she laughed. The other girls trooped in; Mimi, Shoo Shoo, and Loo Loo. I waved them over, and as they approached, I asked my cousin No Name if they could join us.

Mimi asked what we were celebrating, and one of the men said, drinking. The others said nothing, and No Name said, murder.

We drank, then I got reminded that champagne has this tendency to make you go weak in the bladder. If you are not careful, you exhausted the elastic on your panties for taking them down and up, down and up.

I was in the smelly toilet with my panties around my ankles when I heard the noise above the music in the bar. One loud clang, followed by various shouts, people running, chairs, tables and bottles crashing to the floor.

I pulled down my skirt, made to run towards the front and forgot my panties around my ankles. They snapped. Who needs panties anyway?

The veranda was empty, and the new girl with her blood-red blouse stood over the prostrate figure of Big Joe, who must have come in when I was in the toilets. She had something in her hand that looked like a hammer.

Big Joe was like a father to me, even though I gave him the occasional relaxation. Mimi, Shoo shoo, and Loo Loo had plain disappeared, and so had the group at her table.

-We need to get him to a hospital.

She looked at me with that wild dog look, now enhanced by the alcohol. I dragged her to the back of the building.

-You better run back to where ever you came from.

-Do I, do I still remind you of your mother?

She laughed, a laugh I remember. My mother had laughed like that.

-Go, go before the police arrive.

Makaya was empty. Nobody likes being a witness in Victoria. The waiters were still hiding behind the counter, and four newcomers stood at the entrance.

-What happened, what happened?

Useless men. I ran to the road and cried, Taxi!

I sat behind the yellow Toyota to the hospital, cradling Big Joe on my knees, and searched his pockets. I found a wallet and some money, which I secreted in my Wonderbra.

There is a passport in his back pocket. Tucked between the pages of Big Joe's passport, was a picture of a woman smiling into the camera. She was naked. I switched on the ceiling lights in the Taxi. It was not working. My Samsung mobile phone had a torch.

The girl in the picture looked exactly like the new girl. It was her alright, the girl who had walked into Makaya earlier that evening, wearing a blood-red top and grey flannel trousers.

HOW TO GIVE SOUND FINANCIAL ADVICE

One fine January morning, John Ateba is made redundant. He had kept the job for the last seven years, and he rightly thinks it is the end of the world, as he knew it.

It was his first and only job, as a machinist down the umbrella factory at Moliwe, and like anybody losing their first and only thing, he learns it is by no means a good thing to happen to anybody. Especially as that meant, his days of living it up in church street, on beer and roast meat, have to come to an end. So, John Ateba has good reason to feel long in the face, given as jobs of any kind, were particularly hard to come by in his hometown of Victoria.

Indeed, things on the job side of life in Victoria were terrible. Last year, three of his cousins reached the official retirement age guaranteed by law, without ever having the pleasure of a pay check. And they had all been to university.

With jobs of any kind being as rare as fowl's teeth, John mopes about his one-room-and-parlour, and wonders what to do with himself. He does this for a round week.

This long-in-the-face week turns into overflowing joy, when he visits his erstwhile boss out of boredom, and comes into a surprising bit of intelligence.

He learns that, an impressive sum was coming his way by the instrument of redundancy payments. This news cheers him up no end, and he rearranges his position on the point that, unemployment, is a thing that throws water on a man's fire.

He receives the money in crisp clean notes. It was more money than it had ever been his pleasure to see in any one place in all his thirty years on this planet. He resolves to think about what he is to do with so many shiny and crisp notes.

But the feel of half a million francs in new notes, in his back pockets, leaves him unable to focus. It blocks out all thought whatsoever, for two weeks. He was also besieged by fears, real and imagined. He made decisions, and unmade them quicker than the time it took to finish a bottle of export. He only found peace, when he transfers the money to a space between his mattress and the floor of his bed,

One decision lingered, though. It was a resolve that he must not, even under pain and duress, reveal to any friend, or foe, that he was the richest among their lot. As his friends were not likely to take kindly to this intelligence, this was innovative thinking. They may start imagining of all kinds of hostile manoeuvres towards his person and his cash. Particularly, his cash.

So, John Ateba goes below ground for two weeks. He avoids visits to Church Street, as is the custom amongst his peers. This undercover move was to convey intelligence that he had no money. But shunning the exquisite pleasures that abound in Church Street Victoria was not easy. But he was a man of strong will, when he so desired.

John's below ground profile is such a roaring success, that his mates begin to suspect he has lost his job. And not only that, he has left town altogether, to hide his poverty, as was the custom in old Victoria.

But hiding, like lying, was hard to keep up. His neighbour, Mola Never Never, knocks on his door one morning. He had heard movement from within. He asks as follows,

-Neighbour, what is the trouble? For two weeks now, you sleep all day and then sleep some more all night.

John gives him the first part of the story. That of losing the job at the Moliwe umbrella factory, but, he keeps the second part underground, that of receiving half a million in shiny notes.

He keeps the redundancy silent to the neighbour, and so lies by omission. But that was not because his neighbour would not take kindly to this knowledge, but because Mola Never Never, his neighbour, would not understand. Redundancy payments were something which John himself only half understood.

-You can always come work with me on the farm. You know it's not such lousy living after all.

This news is by no means agreeable to John. Particularly the bit about farming being not such lousy living at all. John Ateba could not think of anything worse than farming. In his mind, the only way of making a living was by applying the skills he had learnt from the government technical school in Ombe. He tells the neighbour what he thinks in no uncertain terms.

-So what're you going to do then?

-I don't know; I'll think about it.

- Do think about the farm.

-Well, when a cow has no tail, God takes care of the flies.

He tells his neighbour with words borrowed from the Prince Nico song topping the charts in old Victoria. John does not think about farming, but he believes that he is not a cow, and he has no business with a tail.

That evening, being a Friday, John pays a visit to his friend Sweet Mop Sam, who lives down Nambeke street behind the slaughter house.

Sweet Mop acquired the name from his ability to sweet-talk anyone, especially in the department of telling people what they want to hear. Sweet Mop Sam is also a tailor by profession, and general adviser on all leisure matters.

That is why John finds him engaged in cutting fabric, and speaks to him like this.

- Sweet Mop, hypothetically speaking, which means that it is not true, but only a supposition. If a man has half a million francs, and takes out ten thousand, and spends it in Church Street. Does that action affect the original amount, or does it not?

Sweet Mop leaves his scissors to hang in the air for a bit and a minute, and considers the matter with all the intelligence he could muster. He scratches his head, shoulder, and bottom. Then he replies to John like this.

-No. my very good friend John Ateba. The original amount does not move at all.

-You sure?

-Cannot be surer.

-Get dressed then my friend. I'll come get you at seven. There's a place to which you and I must go.

That evening, the two friends put on their best rags., hit the lights of Church Street. They ate a lot of roast cow, had plenty to drink, and generally made jolly jolly.

John wakes the following day to a bang on his door. It is his neigh-bour Mola Never Never.

-My neighbour, Mola Never Never says. I hate seeing you sleeping your days away. Now, I've been thinking, and I've a little proposi-tion for you.

John rubs his eyes, and lets out a long yawn.

-I've got some money put aside for my daughter's christening.

When John says nothing, Mola Never Never continues. He speaks like a man in a hurry, afraid that if he does not say what he has to communicate quickly, he might never say it.

-I could advance this christening money to you as a small soft loan, and you can start a small business selling cigarettes and sweets.

-Cigarettes and sweets?

-Yes, why not? Many school children like sweets. They pass in front of our house to go to school.

-So, you want to lend me some money?

-Yes. There is no doubt that you will make a success of it and repay my money in less than six months.

John would hear of no such thing, and he tells his appreciation of the kindness so offered. No, he would not take advantage of the kindness and financial advice provided.

For the next six months, John alternates between putting the same question to Sweet Mop Sam, and getting the head and bottom scratching, after which Sweet mop Sam would confirm that the original amount is not at all affected.

Every other week, Mola Never Never knocks on his door and puts forward one useless business proposal after the other. He even included opening a beer parlour in church street, given as beer drinking is what the men of Victoria do.

Six months roll on by, and John Ateba's money dwindles. What with paying rents and getting to know some very fine ladies in Church street. He was also very engaged with Sweet Mop Sam in the getting-drunk business and offering beer to complete strangers, on his own redundancy money. Something which the inhabitants of Victoria called Alcohol-Induced-Generosity, AIG

So, a while later, when John puts the question to Sweet Mop Sam.

-Sweet Mop, hypothetically speaking, which means that it is not true, but only a supposition. If a man has fifty thousand francs, and takes out ten thousand, and spends it in Church Street. Does that action move the original amount or not?

And Sweet Mop Sam says. the original amount does not move at all.

-You lie!!

John shouts. His gives Sweet Mop a swine-blow. They roll about in the dust, and John knocks off two front teeth from Sweet Mop Sam's mouth.

This was out of character, but the residents of New Town considered it, justified.

What Sweet Mop Sam did not know, was that earlier that morning, John Ateba had discovered the space under his mattress was empty of half a million francs. In fact, it was bereft of a franc. Surprised discovery, which he made known to all his neighbours, and the entire population of New Town Victoria.

Sweet Mop Sam later spoke in his own defence as follows.

-If he'd told me of the redundancy money, I would've given him some sound financial advice. I would've advised to open an off-license, a tailoring workshop, or even a very small business, like selling cigarettes and sweets to schoolchildren.

THE DAY MAMI WATA APPEARED IN ETAY ROBERT'S BARBER'S SHOP

Etay Robert's barbershop definitely stood at the end of our street in Gardens Victoria, but there was some argument amongst the boys on my street and those from the road after it, concerning whether it was at our end or at the beginning of theirs. When the council built the public tap and labelled the street as Before Tap, it settled the barbershop location as After Tap. It also decided the place of the curious incident with Pa Jingo.

Etay Robert's barbershop, was a blue and white little wooden shack with a display board painted by Agogo, who definitely lives at the end of my street. The display board, had heads with hairstyles ranging from the "punk salute" to the "agogo-special". The head that carried the Agogo special looked like the artist, Agogo himself, except he had left out the protruding parietal to the back.

Old men played draughts, placed bets on the football pools and drank beer whilst waiting for turns at the Barber's chair. The chair was an old revolving type with holes in the brown plastic sheet. It faced a fading mirror to which the Barber held a smaller mirror behind your back, so you could see the back of your head.

The boys on my street would tell the story of Pa Jingo with authority. After all, it happened on our tuft, and what better authority did anyone need?

The story changed over time, got blown out of proportion. Saucy details got added, but anybody in Gardens could always be relied on to tell it as it was, and point to the barbershop with pride. Years later, Etay Robert died. They knocked down the shop and replaced it with the Deeper Life Gospel Church, but the people on my street would still point to the church and say,

-That's the barbershop where it happened.

It happened at about four in the evening. The sun had burnt itself out by this time. It's light remained, without the fire, as I crossed the culvert the council built only last week unto my street. The barbershop had the usual collection of old men playing draughts.

I had put down my school bag to learn a few moves, before going home, when Etay Robert came running out of his shop with his clipper in one hand. On the other hand, he held the white-brown apron he usually hung around your neck.

The running Etay Robert kicked over the draughts board and fell panting to the ground. The draughts players, two other onlookers and I, scrambled to safety over the culvert to the other side of the street.

-Barber, what's the matter?

Pa Bosco called from a safe distance. Barber crawled to where we were standing and pointed back to his shop.

-Just go in there, and see with your own eyes. He muttered and picked himself up from the ground.

-What're we supposed to see?

All Etay Robert could do, was point to his shop. We looked, but the door blind blocked our view.

-Look, Barber, if this is a joke, you better stop it. You're making my heart jump about like a grasshopper. Papa Bosco said.

Papa Bosco was a big burly man, who worked as a carpenter with the Zoo in Bota and danced the elephant dance during national day celebrations. He had huge biceps, and when he got angry, he flipped his chest muscles up and down through his white string vest.

-Seriously, Barber, I'm ashamed of you. Where is Jingo?

Barber pointed to his shop.

-You mean Jingo is still in there?

Jingo was the oldest resident of our street. He lived alone under a big mango tree, which produced the most prominent fruits in Victoria. His fruits were so out of the ordinary, that neighbours with mango trees with smaller fruits, said he danced naked at night under it to make the fruits grow to their unusual size. His wife disappeared last Christmas with the children, and some said, it was the dance that had done it.

We never saw him dance, but the dance was one of those things that needed no proof. Etay Robert cut Jingo's hair to the skin every Friday and left a round patch of red-black hair on the top. Barber always applied an excellent lick of palm kennel oil to the areas where the skin showed, and you could see your face at the back of his head, when he took his turn at the draughts board.

Pa Bosco inched towards the entrance of the barbershop. We watched him go past the signboard with the heads, and gripped the dirty brown cloth that gave Etay Robert's clients some privacy. Pa Bosco tore it down, and inched inside the shop.

We all moved to the barbershop side of the street. Just when we were about to think it was safe, Pa Bosco came running out, and tripped over one of the former draughts players' upturned stool.

-What is it? What is it?

There was a crowd now. Barber and Pa Bosco sat on the ground, and shook their heads.

-Look, somebody said, are you guys chickens, or what?

-Just go in there and see for yourself.

Barber muttered, whilst Pa Bosco shrugged his shoulders.

-Is he still in there? Asked one of the men who had played draughts with Pa Bosco a few minutes ago.

Pa Bosco looked to the ground.

-Is it Mami Wata?

The crowd took turns firing questions, and before long, everybody was speaking at once, and Pa Bosco shook his head to every question.

-Is it a mboma?

A shake of the head.

-How can Jingo turn into Mami Wata and a snake, at the same time?

Pa Bosco looked at Barber, who stared at the ground. But despite this ground look, an invisible thread linked them.

Before our eyes, they became the only people in the world who had seen something never seen by another person, living or dead.

I felt a hand on my ear. As my mother pulled me away, somebody at the edge of the crowd said,

-Pa Jingo has turned into a crocodile with Mammy water's head, inside Etay Robert's barbershop.

We were to know the true story later when Barber found his tongue, but by then, the story had taken on many heads. Pa Bosco never spoke about what he saw, at least not to my hearing. But the inhabitants of Gardens, notwithstanding the various reports of what actually happened, never argued about one thing. This thing was, what Etay Robert saw, was very different from what Pa Bosco saw.

THE BETRAYAL

When my second eldest brother Joshua returned from America, he did three things, the retelling of which, entered into the family narrative.

The first, attracted the behind-the-back disapprobation of my mother, father, and Auntie. Our eldest brother Obadiah was not very happy neither. The second, taught me a thing or two, and the third, flowed from the second, and set me down a path to a course of action I would regret to my dying day.

Joshua touched down at the Douala International Airport after an absence of three years. He had forgotten to inform us he was coming, and deprived our family of the pleasure of waiting for him at the airport. As if that was not enough, he went up to Bambili, and married Juanita, whom he had met as a teenage student up-country.

When he heard of the wedding, our father jumped up and down, called his ancestors to witness his disgrace, and asked, who represented his family at the wedding. After that, he took to mentioning his blood pressure more than the usual two times a day. My mother tut-tut-ted behind Josh's back, and my auntie asked to Joshua's face, what my father and everybody could not ask.

-How did you know she's a good girl?

Back then in Victoria, it did not matter if the girl were fat, thin, short, tall, thief or child molester, so long as she was good.

When my auntie Marianna asked that ultimate question, I wanted to inquire what a good girl meant. But the worry lines on my auntie's face, discouraged any honest inquiry.

To make things worse, she asked the good or not good question, in front of Juanita. Juanita smiled her incomprehension. The question had come out in the language of a tribe which was not her own, but I suspected she got the drift, as contrary to popular belief, a person could always tell when they were the subject of a conversation, irrespective of the language in which they made the subject of the sentence.

Joshua did not give our auntie an answer. She was our mother's only sister, and she had no children of her own. In Victoria, you never gave lippy answers back to your only auntie. When Juanita returned to her people, he confided to my eldest brother and me when we sat at dinner one day.

As we dug in, he told us why he was sure he not only loved his Juanita, but knew she was the best of all good girls.

-You see; the thing was exactly how I left it, four years ago.

I did not know what he meant, but Obadiah, who was swallowing at the time, nearly choked on his food.

-How do you know? Obadiah spluttered.

-When I say the thing was exactly how I left it, I know it's exactly how I left it.

This conversation was way above my head.

-I don't understand, I ventured.

-You see, it's like this. Joshua started, addressing me.

-You know when Mama used to serve us rice and stew?

-Yes, I said.

-And you would hide yours in the cupboard to eat later?

-Yes?

I wondered where my big brother was going with this line of questioning, but he has been all over the world, and knows a thing or two.

-Imagine you came back, and Obadiah has taken a spoonful of your rice and stew.

-Yes? I said, and glanced at Obadiah, urging him to remember the many times he pinched my rice and stew.

-You would know, wouldn't you?

With that, he left the room, and Obadiah, whom father has been harassing for three years to move out, get a job, and look for a good girl, said,

-Look. Never ever trust a woman, and that Joshua, for all his book sense, is a Mougou.

-But, said I, I always know when somebody has touched my rice and stew.

-Look, little brother, when a canoe goes over water, does it leave a track?

-Yes. I replied, seeing the white watery wake.

-But, for how long?

I had spent many an afternoon, watching outboard engine boats down the docks, and knew how long the wake took.

A Mougou as an idiot. The name did not sit well on Joshua. He had been to America and back, Obadiah has never left Victoria, not even to the Douala airport. Now, we all suspected Obadiah was jealous of Joshua, and my auntie confirmed it later that evening.

-Rubbish.

She cried, when I recounted Joshua's story. Don't mind Obadiah. He needs to hurry and get married. That girl is good.

-So you now think she's a good girl?

-Why not? All women are good.

-That's not what father thinks. His blood pressure has gone up because of Juanita.

-Don't worry about your father. He'll be okay. Did you see what Joshua brought me from America?

She showed me. A t-shirt with MOTOWN scrawled across the front of her ample belly.

Years later, when I was to travel to Italy, I remembered that conversation. I remembered Joshua, who now had three American children with the good Juanita.

-You'll wait for me? I asked Lucy.

-Of course, you know, since I met you....

Of course, she was a good girl. My heart did little summersaults every time I saw her. When she put her sweet little soft fingers on mine, jolts of electricity went up and down my arm, down my belly, and down between my legs.She was good, but did Obadiah not say one should never trust a woman?

-An oath is what we need, Lucy said three days before my departure.

-A pledge will settle your doubts.

-Swear on the bible?

-No, that's not strong enough; I know this medicine man. My uncle went to see him, just before he left for Germany.

Now, if a sweet girl like Lucy was prepared to go all that way, to show me she would wait for me, I was not going to argue.

We found the medicine man, I paid the fee, and we pricked our fingers, chewed some herbs, and it was settled.

-If any of you break this oath, it's instant death. Do you understand?

He ran his right index finger across his throat, from left to right. His bloodshot eyes lingered on my face, then on Lucy's and then back to me. Cold sweat broke all over my back. I swallowed hard.

-But, no, nobody said anything about death.

I muttered. The Medicine man asked Lucy to wait outside, and turned his red beady eyes on me.

-You're a man, and she is a woman.

He said in the tone my father uses when he wants to tell us not to listen to our mother.

-Yes.

-We're men, we are different from women.

-Yes.

-Okay, you can come back anytime, and I'll undo the oath for free, but for now, this's what you'll do.

He gave me a bundle in a brown piece of paper, tied with yellow thread.

-This is the antidote.

I rolled the bundle over in my hands.

-When your flesh fails, take one grain immediately after the failure.

-Take it?

-Yes, chew it, chew it seven times, and then swallow.

Sweat broke all over my fore head. It dripped to the earthen floor, covered with blood-red camwood paste. Outside, a cock crowed, and Lucy waited.

-This is between you and me. There's no need to tell your little girlfriend about it.

And I did not.

In the years I was away, my body was weak, often, and I stuck to his prescription. More than one girl asked me, why I had to rush to the bathroom after every time, and I gave a quick line about needing a glass of water. If any of them wondered why I did not use the kitchen, they never said.

And I would have continued like that if I had not met Leonita, and with her, it was not only my body that was weak, my heart was as well. I could not keep relying on my dwindling supplies of bittersweet seeds, from a medicine man back in New Town Victoria.

At the end of four years, I returned to Victoria, and fell into Lucy's arms again, and I understood what my brother had meant about knowing if somebody had pinched my food.

I was not due back for another two years, was already tiring of the tiny seeds; and what was more, I knew I could not control my heart anymore. Leonita had moved from my dreams to waking moments with Lucy, so I made a secret journey to the medicine man.

He had not changed in all that time.

-So, what do you want now?

-I want out. I want to break the oath.

-What? Tired so soon?

-Yes, I'm tired.

-And the seeds, they worked? I didn't let you down.

-No, you didn't, but I don't want it anymore.

-Guilt, eh?

-Nothing to do with guilt.

-Well, you'll have to bring the girl along.

Now, there was no way I was going to drag sweet Lucy back here. What explanation would I give?

-That's your problem, said the medicine man, now, for a million francs, I'll undo the oath.

I had come with no money, and even if I had, not that kind of money.

-I've no money, and you said it would be free…

He laughed. I could not see the joke. Through peals of laughter, he said.

-So, you believed me?

-Yes, I believed you. And you said, you'd never betray the trust we put in you.

I hoped by agreeing, he might just soften and undo the spell.

-You're dumber than you look. You're a Mougou.

My head spun.

-Go and find that stupid girl, she might have been foolish enough, to wait for you all this time.

-But I don't....

-You don't what?

-I met this other girl, Leonita...

He laughed so hard, rolled on the blood-red camwood floor. He carried on laughing on the floor, and I worried, he would choke.

-I said, a million francs! And if I were that girl, I wouldn't marry you, for anything in the world.

-Why would you say that?

-Because, because, you're a Mougou.

-Stop calling me that!

-A million francs, or your life. Unless, you can keep to an oath, and then it'll be free.

DR DO GOOD

It is the first day of the term, after the short break.

In the wooden class five B of Our lady of Lourdes Catholic school in Gardens Victoria, the boys in Khaki shorts and sky blue shirts, and the girls in sky blue dresses trimmed with white at the neck, settle down in their seats, amidst shouts, whispers and paper planes flying overhead.

The class teacher Mister Jerome raps on the blackboard with his cane, and a hushed silence fills the classroom. There was a firm catholic belief in my school, as unquestioned as our belief in the infallibility of the Pope, that if you got the cane on the first day of term, your future was sealed. The rest of the term will follow in the same pattern.

We fall silent, not out of respect for his teacher status, but because Mister Jerome has a weapon. It is the cane.

The cane was real; the teacher was not. The cane had sucked up whatever respect we had for Mister Jerome. It also had a name, Dr do good.

The children in class two B opposite, fill the silence that followed the cane rap, with a song about a chariot coming to take them home.

Story telling time! Teacher Jerome announces

It is my turn to tell a story to the class. I stumble on unsteady legs to the front, and hastily tuck in my shirt into my Khaki breeches. I check the flat piece of Dunlop I had sewn to the seats of my shorts. The thin Dunlop was both defence against Dr Do Good, and also respect for his august person.

I turn around to face the class, and stifled laughter hits me somewhere in the stomach, from the left of the room.

Mirabelle sits to the left of the room, so, I say a silent prayer. I could take laughter from anybody, but not from her.

Mister Jerome raps again on the board, and another silence descends. He points to the front of my khaki shorts, with Dr Do good. I look down trembling, and realise one shirt flap was still sticking out. I rearrange it.

I clear my throat,

-One day…

Mister Jerome raps on the board again.

-That's not how you start a story.

He had taught us a fixed opening to telling stories. I arrange my shirt flaps and tails, and bring my ankles together. I do not know where to put my hands, so I plunge them into my pockets. There is a hole in the left one, and I wriggle my index finger through it.

I restart, following the formula.

-Arabian Nights.

The whole class throats back at me.

-Entertainment.

-Boys and girls, I want to tell you a story.

-Yes, we are ready to hear your story, what is your story about?

-My story is about, one day, there was a man. He had two children, John and Mary.

Somebody to the back of the class gives a shout, and a little apple rolls to the floor. Mister Jerome, whose head had dropped when I said the Arabian nights bit, raises it from his teacher's table, and grabs Dr do good.

-Who threw down that apple?

There is complete silence. Mr Jerome picks up the offending apple, walks up and down the aisles of the three rows in the classroom with an apple in one hand, and Dr do good in the other.

-What is this?

-An apple! Somebody shouts back.

-And what do we know about apples?

-Eve gave one to Adam.

-Yes, the source of good, and evil.

Mister Jerome stops in front of Tom. Tom raises his hands to cover his head. The teacher turns, and marches back to his post behind the table in front of the blackboard. He turns to me with Dr do good.

-Continue.

And then to the rest of the class,

-If I hear a little squeak from any of you, you will smell Dr do good.

Silence.

-What would you smell?

Silence again. Not even the bravest, wanted to smell Dr do good. Not on the first day of term.

Mister Jerome waves Dr do good in the air.

-What would you smell?

The rattling cane has the desired effect. The whole class bellows back, like one man.

-Dr do good.

-Good, Mister Jerome says, now get on with the story, and we want a story about the New Year.

Outside, it is hot, the sun blazes down, and a dog chases a chicken across the handball pitch.

-Arabian Nights?

The whole class throats back at me.

-Entertainment.

-Boys and girls, I want to tell you a story.

They throat back,

-Yes, we are ready to hear your story, what is your story about?

-My story is about, one day, there was a woman, and she had two children, John and Mary.

Mister Jerome lifts his head and says in a thick voice,

-The story should be about the New Year.

The thickness of his voice, is from the maize and beans porridge we know he eats every day, at Mammy Cecilia down in Church Street.

I clear my throat and start again.

-My story is about, one day there was a woman, and she had two children, John and Mary. And the woman had promised each, a new pair of shoes, for the New Year.

I look at Mister Jerome, and he nods his approval.

-But this woman had no husband, and no money. So, she thought hard and long, on how she was going to get money, to buy shoes for John and Mary. Since she had no husband, she decides to sell apples.

I look over to Mister Jerome, and he snores lightly back at me. Somebody whispers to the back of the class.

-How come, she has no husband?

The snore is now audible. Dr do good too, snores silently on Mr Jerome's table.

-Well, she had no husband, I say.

-Then. how did she have children?

It is Ethan. He wants to spoil my story. The whole class jumps about in their seats.

-Well, I say, Mammy Cecilia has no husband, but she has two children.

The class goes hush again, as if Dr do good were circling above the hot smelly air. Somebody, Ethan I think, shouts,

-How can she have children, without a husband?

-I don't know, I shout back.

-Everyone has a father. Somebody says.

-Maybe she is an Ashawo. Ethan says.

A paper aeroplane lands at my feet. I pick it up, and somebody had scrawled on it,

-Mister Jerome, is the father of Mammy Cecelia's children.

I consider this for a moment. One of her boys is called Jerome.

-Is Mister Jerome the father? I ask.

The class erupts. Mr Jerome wakes up from his siesta, and grabs Dr do good.

-Can, anybody tell me, what's the meaning of all this?

He stares at the class with sleep red eyes. Not a squeak, not a breeze passes. Somehow, we knew we have crossed the forbidden river. Outside, the dog and the chicken have disappeared from the handball pitch.

-Please sir.

It was Ethan. He stands.

-Goddy says, Mammy Cecilia is an Ashawo, and she will use Ashawo to buy New Year clothes for her children.

Mister Jerome turns to me.

-What is an Ashawo?

-An Ashawo is a prostitute.

-Shut up, Ethan!

Mr Jerome looks at me, like he is seeing me for the first time, deciding whether I am friend, or a foe. I glance at Dr do good.

-Which Mammy Cecilia?

Ethan answers in my place.

-The one who sells beans in Church Street.

I did not say Mammy Cecilia was an Ashawo, and I am not going to let my good name be sullied.

-It's a lie. I said my story is about, a woman who had no husband, and then somebody said...

Before I could finish, I hear Dr do good rushing towards my buttocks. He lands with a thud on my Dunlop pad, and the class erupts in jubilation. First day of the first term in the New Year.

-What have you got in your hand?

I give it to him.

-Somebody threw it, I swear, that's not my handwriting.

Mister Jerome is shaking, like a man who has malaria. He turns to the class.

-I swear; it is not my hand writing.

-Shut up!

I shut up. Mr Jerome turns to the class.

-Everyone, stand up, and line up against that wall.

They all line up.

-Ethan, you, come to the front and grab the table.

We knew the drill.

Mr Jerome usually tires progressively. The first in line gets the full energy of his beans and maize. I pray to Mathew, Mark, Luke and John. Please let it be that Ethan forgot to slip a flat piece of Dunlop, down the seat of his khaki shorts.

A WOMAN OF SUBSTANCE

It was Mola Likoka who first introduced me to the concept of women of substance. He did so, when making a negative indictment on my most recent unsuccessful amorous adventure.

-Why don't you go out with the young professional women in town?

-Professional women?

-Yeah, lawyers, teachers, women of substance.

-Why?

-It would be less tedium than the university students you seem to take a shine to.

I was twenty-four, fresh out of university, and up until then, I had found nothing wrong with dating a university girl.

-You need a woman who makes their own money.

-But I don't want their money.

-I know that, but think about it. You don't need to take a woman of substance out to a chicken dinner, to impress them.

-But, I don't buy chicken, and I am not looking to impress anybody.

-Think about it, you'll spend less money, and save a few chickens.

In Victoria, the chicken was king, the love lubricator of choice. It was not often that a young girl turned down an invitation to eat fish, or chicken. Particularly chicken.

In the first twelve months since I came back to Victoria, I had bought so many chicken dinners at the Mars bar, I could have built a small house in Motowor with the money.

Mola Likoka 's words were not unattractive to me.

I thought about the women I knew, who I did not need to buy a chicken dinner on the first date. There was no denying there were young pretty twenty-something teachers in the secondary schools. Government high school boasted a few. Saker Baptist college too, had a couple. But the young lawyers and doctors, were either too old, too dull, or just did not have the vava voom I was looking for at that age.

I thought some more about my conversation with Mola Likoka for a couple of weeks, and settled on giving it a try. I set about getting to know the women of substance in Victoria, and started with this teacher down the Presbyterian Girls school, next to Pressbook. I cornered her one day after school.

-Ermm, excuse me, do you mind if I...

She brushed me off.

-Look, if you're trying to chat me up, let me tell you, I only go out with people your father's age, and they must have money to pay my rent.

I was not really that into her, so, I said

-Those rich old men must have abysmal taste.

That was not a nice thing to say, but somebody had to say it. She was a big girl, built like a boxer, with hair on her chin. My paramour, the one Mola Likoka, disapproved of was Miss universe in comparison, and it made better financial sense to buy chicken, if the other side was to pay rents.

I gave up on these women of substance, and carried on with first dates of chicken and roast fish.

Then one day, I ran into Maureen at the post office counter. We had both come to pick up registered letters. She was a history teacher up at Saker Baptist college, and pretty in the way pretty was considered in Victoria. She was not into old men, I guessed, because she lived in college accommodation, and did not have to worry about rents.

-Why don't we do drinks on Saturday?

No mention of chicken.

-Why not? She laughed. I could cook for you beforehand?

Now, this was very promising. Since I returned to Victoria, my mother was the only woman who had cooked for me. It would look as if this woman of substance thing was unfolding rather well. It definitely had something going for it.

-What's your favourite food?

This was even more interesting. My favourite food was Ekpang, cooked with lobsters and half dried barracuda.

-Hmm, she said. You're a man of rather expensive tastes.

I agreed that I was.

-Here, I said, I'll contribute some to the costs of dried barracuda.

-Seven o'clock sharp.

We shook hands on seven o'clock. This was the time when they had just introduced the new two thousand franc note, and because it was new, the banks made it a law to distribute as many as possible. I had gone to the bank only the other day, and my purse was bulging with them. I presented her with two.

I turned up at her house on the appointed Saturday, at seven o'clock sharp. It was a lovely sitting room, with cross-stitch head rests on every sofa. The overhead electric bulb had been shaded with pink toilet paper, so that the light was soft, atmospheric, conducive to pleasant conversation.

I was liking this woman every minute. But what was more, she had cooked the most excellent Ekpang. If I had any worries that four thousand francs were enough to impress two university girls, they were dispersed by the amount of food on the table.

She served it in a massive serving bowl, enamel metal things you got down in Newtown market, decorated with the head of Murtala Mohamed, the murdered Nigerian president.

I watched her transfer a huge cooking spoonful from the serving bowl. After that, she said Grace, interlaced her fingers and flexed them. Then she dipped four lovely nimble fingers into her plate, picked up a couple of Ekpang rolls laced with barracuda, and carried them to her mouth. She ate heartily, one of those people who, watching them eat, made you hungry as well.

-Come on eat, eat, there is plenty.

I complied. If I say it was the best Ekpang I have had the pleasure of eating all my life, it was not an understatement. Within an hour, we had had, between us, enough of it to last me a lifetime. But there was a downside to so much eating. My stomach was not as elastic as it used to be, and it complained at the excess.

-I am so full, my stomach hurts. I said.

-Ah, poor you. Let me see.

She walked over to my side of the table.

-Go on, lift your shirt, and let me see.

She prodded my belly with the fingers she had used for the Ekpang. It was as taut as a new skin over a drum.

-Do you want some Andrew's liver salts?

No, I did not. I had heard people did that, and I know of some who ate, and vomited their food to create space for more food. Somehow, the Catholic in me said it was barbaric, a near sin.

No, I was not going to stoop that low. But I had a more pressing difficulty, and it was that, it was impossible to cuddle anybody when both your stomachs were stretched to explosion point.

Just then, I had a brilliant idea.

-Why don't we get some brandy instead?

-Instead?

-Yes instead of doing beers. It's rather good for digestion,

-Whoopee, she said. I love brandy, but where do we find it in Victoria at this time?

At the time, the was country man's bar in church street, but I kept quiet about that. Besides, I did not want to leave her company, get a taxi down town, and run the risk of meeting one of my old reliables, who never cooked Ekpang. They might not take kindly to the news; I was on a date without them. I then said,

-Let's go to the SS club.

The Senior Service club was on the other side of town, after the palm oil mill. The British had built it in an attempt to introduce the concept of class, to a place where money was the only determinant of class. In the old days, it was the refuge of the oil plantations' management staff, a place where they could escape the smell of palm oil, and pretend to be uppity.

If there was any more excellent place in all Victoria to take in the sea breeze, and digest Ekpang whilst sipping on a glass of brandy, I did not know of it.

We hailed a taxi.

-Two for Bota.

-Two hundred francs, the driver said.

When we arrived, I discovered the smallest denomination in my purse, was a two thousand franc note. The driver scratched his head and spat out of the window.

-Should've said, you had only notes. You know the problem with change.

He had a point there. The people who ran the Central bank never gave any thought to the amount of each denomination they put into circulation.

-My brother, I thought I had a two-hundred-franc coin on me.

-You should've checked.

The driver would not entertain the idea of Maureen and I walking into the club, as we might never come out again. So, I dashed in, leaving Maureen as a hostage.

The barman could not lend me two-hundred-francs.

-You are the first person to walk in today.

-Really?

-We have no takings.

He opened the empty cash till.

I walked slowly back to the taxi, hoping a friend might just wander past, but I had no satisfaction. If Maureen had any reservations at being left as a two-hundred-franc hostage, she did not show it. I leaned on the driver's window and said,

-There is no change.

My date sat quiet, watching with bemusement, our exchange. The driver sighed and said,

-I have to take you back to where I picked you.

-Hey, hang on, I begged, you could drop us here, and then tomorrow, I swear, I'll look for you, and give you the two hundred with interest.

-So you think I'm a fool?

I lost my temper at that point, and told him he was a little twerp of a miserable man.

The little twerp drove us back to where he had picked us in New Town. We then spent about an hour looking for change. When we found it, we caught another taxi back to Bota.

SS club was rather lovely. You did not find any of the rowdy hoi polloi you get in the other watering holes in Victoria. And besides, the cook, Kenneth was my buddy. We had grown up together in Gardens.

When our order arrived, she began to tell me about her work, complained about the school principal, and drank brandy under a fluorescent bulb. I was still on my first glass, when she ordered her third. This was a strange way to discover women of substance made for costly first dates. But hey, I did not expect her to drink Top Grenadine, like the university girls, and the brandy had been my idea.

She then asked for a fourth serving. When it arrived, she smacked her lips on the rim of her glass, and said,

-I have a funny feeling in my throat.

-It's all that Ekpang we ate.

-No. I don't think so. I believe it's the brandy.

-The brandy?

-Yes.

-Then, you shouldn't drink so much of it.

I was worried about the dent she was putting in my stash of two thousand franc notes. Then she pushed the boat out some more.

-I think I need something pepperish.

My heart fell.

Something pepperish was the name the university students had given to roast meat and chicken, and the SS club had a reputation for chicken and meat pies, but the meat pies did not come with pepper. The chicken did.

-It's just the pepper I want. She insisted.

Then I had a light bulb moment. My man Kenneth was in the kitchen. I said,

-Let me see if they have any pepper left.

I found Kenneth throwing chicken quarters into a deep fat frying pan. In exchange for a bottle of export in Atabong's in Gardens the next day, he agreed to walk to our table, and tell my date, there was no pepper left in the kitchen.

Kenneth was excellent. She listened to him, played with the ends of her Brazilian wig, and rolled her eyes to the moth beating against fluorescent bulb.

-You mean, there's no pepper?

-Yes.

-No pepper in a senior service club?

-Yes Madam.

-What kind of place is this?

My homeboy Kenneth, was buttering it up nicely. His use of the word madam, was a nice touch. I made a mental note to make use of it next time.

-Let me see. Maureen said, and looked up at the ceiling as if to see something up there. Just when I thought I had won, she said, addressing Kenneth,

-I tell you what, just, just bring the chicken without the pepper.

Kenneth glanced at me. This was not part of our plan, and it was difficult to say there was no chicken in the club, as we had been filling our lungs all evening, with roast and fried chicken. Mola Lokoko was wrong with this woman of substance thing. This one was costing more in an evening, than three university girls did in a month.

She ordered three portions and ate like she had not eaten in three weeks. My stomach still ached, from overeating earlier in the evening, and watching her, made me nauseous.

-How can you eat so much in one night?

If I thought she would take offence, I was wrong.

-I like chicken, and besides, chicken is not food?

-Not food? What is it then?

-Chicken is, chicken, is enjoyment.

The imperative for polite conversation had evaporated. I finished my drink in silence. When we were about to leave, she asked for

Kenneth.

-What do you want this time? I asked, feigning politeness, but my voice came out wrong. She tilted her chin towards me.

-Meat pies.

The meat pies in the SS club, were legendary. But this was way, way too far out. I could not contain myself any longer.

-Baby, I don't think I have enough money to pay for the brandy, the chicken, and some meat pies as take away.

-Aww, my baby, do not worry, I only want two meat pies. They are a hundred francs each, are they not?

I shook my head.

-I have the money here. Take, two hundred francs.

THE SHORT AND AMAZINGLY BEAUTIFUL LIFE OF JOE MASSANGO.

The final resting place of young Joe Massango, is well-hidden on the far eastern slope of the municipal graveyard in the lush township of old Victoria. It is tucked behind the Catholic Church with its blue and red stained glass windows, and yellow mud-splattered walls. It is a hidden place of peace on the forest border. From this place, the forest climbs a hill still virgin and innocent.

The residents of Victoria, those given to looking upwards, can see the hill from the westernmost end of Church Street, but few knew what lay at its feet.

A casual walker in the graveyard, will see weed-assaulted broken wooden crosses, which marked the graves of erstwhile residents of Victoria. If they carried on walking towards the forest fringe, they will eventually descend a low spear grassed slope, past a moss-covered concrete temple to a dearly beloved, and arrive at an apparition, like an oasis in a desert.

This apparition, is an oblong mound of earth, underneath which lies Joe Massango. Neither wooden cross nor marble-excess, marks the spot. But it is covered by a riot of flowers. The casual walker will find; yellow hibiscus, red rose periwinkles, white lilies, red Johnny walkers, and the occasional bird of paradise. This same casual walker, may never understand how, or why the flowers got here.

Few citizens of Victoria wandered this far, and remained blissfully unaware of its existence.

Though they might not know of this flower-covered grave, they knew Joe all right. And would not care to remember, how he came to rest below this flower-strewn mound. In some way, Joe was responsible for the disdain with which the residents of Victoria still heap on the people of Kumba.

The reason for this was two-fold. Joe was not born in Victoria, but watered farther up the coast on the other side of the mountain, which stands above the town of old Victoria, like an avenging angel,

The story of Joe Masango began in Hausa quarters Fiango, in that old hell hole town of Kumba. He was conceived after his father said, rollover, and his mother did.

Despite Kumba being a hell hole, Joe grew solid and quick, so that by the time he was nineteen, he had learnt there was easy pickings amongst his neighbours. Not all of them mind you, not those who worked at the local Cocoa Marketing Board sorting depot. Those, were not old, and rich.

He was no thief, nor burglar, nor low down gutter scoundrel, after the clean meaning of the words. But in his not so earthly paradise of Kumba, he took property from people, people in whom, he never showed any interest, never asked for permission, and never received any.

This failure to show interest in what people thought about his unauthorised use of their property, was not young Joe's fault. His victims could not talk, were always quiet, and were all dead.

And, because death was the only certainty one can lay any claim to in Kumba, Joe Masango thrived. All who knew him, remarked he was as sheen-faced happy as anyone had a right to be.

Three things enabled Joe Masango to blossom like a tree planted by the rivers of waters. Just like trees need three things: water, sunlight, and nutrients, Joe needed three things. His surroundings provided these.

The first, was a thrift culture bordering on the miserly, amongst the good citizens of Kumba. The second, was a fear of marriage, and its financial demands, which ensured that men invariably married late. The second was linked to the first, because people in Kumba believed that the presence of wives, was iniquitous to thrift. The third, was not unique to Kumba, but was fairly widespread throughout the country. It was the fact that, old men liked marrying young women.

This trinity of custom and practice, in the land where Joe Massango grew tall, robust, and handsome, would provide him with easy living, and would facilitate an early death at the age of thirty-eight in far off Victoria, on the shores of the Atlantic Ocean.

Joe, it turned out, was not too bright at school. He flunked his O levels and gave up after five attempts. He was also not too bright at deciding what to do after school, so he drifted for a couple of years, until he stumbled across Nene, the recently widowed wife of Mister Mesumbe of Buea road.

She met him when she was strolling in her widow's weeds in front of Soba park on Buea road, but that did not stop her from taking a side look at him, his strong broad shoulders, one look at his teeth which reminded her of pearls, though she had never seen a pearl. After that look, she was gone, way gone!

Mister Mesumbe was the local moneylender and richest man in all Kumba, whose wealth was only matched by his age. So when he passed on to the great beyond at the ripe old age of Ninety-eight, he left behind his twenty-five-year-old widow, with what some considered a grave responsibility. That of spending the money he had stashed away so diligently for eighty-odd years.

But unfortunately, she was not given to thinking about this responsibility, and did not know which end of a pig to feed with it, but for the timely intervention of Joe Massango. A tornado-force romance ensued, powered by old Mesumbe's money.

The amount of tongue-wagging that followed, forced the pretty young Nene to move to Douala, where Joe Masango visited intermittently. But Joe would eventually stop, encouraged to do so, by the long travel, and having to speak French, which was something he did not much care for.

But, he had discovered a profitable line in young widows, and there was no turning back.

Joe became the talk of town. His appearances in bars and eating places in Kumba, wearing the latest Julien shirts, cross-stitched pants, and Pierre Cardin shoes, did evince sighs of jealousy. How does he manage to look so good, smell so good, and set the unmarried women to straightening their backs, when he was around?

They had a point there. They knew Joe had no work to talk of, and no rich parents to provide the shirts, shoes and perfume. But it would take them a couple of years to unravel the reason for his obviously beautiful, well dressed, and happy existence. The young widows never complained, because, Joe made them happy. He was welcome relief from a stultifying life married to an old man. He came into their lives and brushed away the cobwebs that had accumulated during their conjugal years.

As it was customary for the living to speak for the dead, the other old men who were still married to young women in Kumba, claimed this right. They claimed the right to ward off what they knew as their eventual fate. So that is how the living old men ganged up, started a rumour that Joe had a capability of hastening their departure to the land of the silent, and chased Joe Masango out of town.

Things got so hot, Joe hotfooted out of town one Sunday evening, and found himself in the leafy sleepy town of Victoria, where he continued his trade without the burden of history.

Joe found the old men of good old Victoria not much different from the old men of Kumba. They too, were in the business of marrying young women, and leaving them young widows, and Joe had a roaring time with this similarity.

He carried on swimmingly, until Mister Babaka, who was as rich as shit, and twice as clever, got to hear about Joe from his brother Pa Simo, who was visiting from Kumba. His brother had seen Joe Massango about drinking Guinness in Church Street, and got alarmed. Pa Simo told his brother of the plague that had befallen the poor old men of Kumba.

Now, Babaka had married a twenty-year-old, when he was seventy. He had saved and scrimped all his life, so when he heard the tale of Joe Massango, he knew he had to take evasive action. His urgency was amplified by the fact that he had seen the grim reaper a couple of times. He had survived, but like they say, you live to die another day.

Mr Babaka decided to act quickly before he answered the reaper's call. The first tool in his tool box, was eating whole pigs in a week, and general merry making, in line with the old wisdom that, what really belonged to a man, was that which he put in his belly.

But too much eating and carrying-on is inimical to business, and it was inevitable that Mr Babaka would neglect his business selling fake jewellery, and sponsoring armed robbers.

He bought clothes and liquor, and generally caught up on the things he had deprived himself, for sixty years.

If his wife had any misgivings on this carrying on of her ever-loving husband, she kept it to herself. She even encouraged it, given that she had nearly died of starvation in her father's house. It was this near-death experience that had informed her decision to marry Mr Babaka.

So, she joined her loving husband in general jollying, grew pretty rotund, and developed high blood pressure and diabetes at a young age.

And as ill-luck would have it, two years into the binge-eating, wanton drinking and business absconding, she choked on a pig trotter and was as dead as a dodo, just about the time when her husband's money had just plain run out.

Now, old Babaka loved his wife, contrary to Victoria opinion, and her sudden death, was the Fako mountain falling on his head. So, the lonely, and heartbroken Mr Babaka was faced with a life of penury, which he blamed on Joe Massango, though the scoundrel of Hausa quarters Kumba had not even set eyes on his wife, dead or otherwise.

Old Babaka decided to square things up, and assuage his conscience. He bought a machete from the Moonchi man down at Big Mop Market in Cassava farms, and filed it so sharp, he could have shaved with it, if he wanted. Then he swallowed a good deal of New Town gin, and began a search high and low, for the unsuspecting Joe.

Mr Babaka eventually found the hapless lad in the arms of the widow of the second richest man in Victoria, Mister Vikedadoo, who had died just a few months earlier from a surfeit of achu soup, dried meat and groundnuts.

The effect of the swinging machete was disastrous, but the widow survived.

The flowers on Joe Massango's grave are the work of this widow, and other young widows of Victoria. The flowers were an appreciation of what they had received, and will now miss, with the extinction of the once beautiful and amazing life of Joe Massango.

HOW TO GET YOURSELF A RICH MAN IN VICTORIA

I first met Diana when she was a thin eleven-year-old, on the school farm of Our lady of Lourdes Roman Catholic school Gardens. Our class was building beds for planting melons. She stood apart from a group of other eleven-year-olds, who swung hoes and pickaxes. She was shouting, with her stance, how different she was, from those who coaxed the hard brown earth loose, and piled them on neat rows to one side.

She was new to Gardens school. She sucked on a lollipop, as she watched them. Diana was neat even back then. The creases on her cheap cotton school uniform, hung straight, the work of a hot charcoal iron. She swayed in time to the fall of the hoes of the bunch of kids who did not have well-ironed school uniforms.

I walked to the mango tree on the edge of the farm, and she joined me in the shade.

-Hey, she said, why are you not working like the others?

-I'm the head boy, and head boys don't work. They supervise.

I said, showing off my expanding lexicon. I took out my punishment book, which I supplied to the teacher after every workday.

-And you what's your excuse, you'll hear from Mister Tanyiko.

 Mister Tanyiko was our new teacher, and had a reputation with the whip.

She laughed, a laugh with echoes of lollipop and ridicule.

-I don't need to work because I'm pretty. You see that boy over there?

I followed her thin tapering fingers covered with lollipop drivel, to Edmund, whose back glistened with sweat.

 -He's making my melon beds for me. I'm not lazy, but you boys can sweat all you like, I'm a pretty girl, and cute girls don't sweat.

She was pretty. I did not know what pretty meant at that age, but there was something about her dark eyes, and the shape of her mouth, that I took to mean pretty.

-A lazy man will end up in prison. I said.

She threw down her Lollipop stick and pushed it into the earth with her toe.

-My mother says, it's important to prepare myself for when I marry a rich man. I need soft hands.

-Soft hands?

-Yes, and he'll get me everything I need. You know rich men like pretty girls with soft hands.

I did not know that.

-Who told you?

-What?

-About rich men, and...

-Oh, my mother did.

She left me in the shade, walk over to Edmund. She said something. His hoe stopped in an arc over his head, and he let out a strangled laugh. The other boys joined in.

Later, none of them could tell me what she had said, that was so funny.

The following term, I gave her a bird. I had found it in one of the traps behind the school church. It was beautiful, and it was alive. Its wings were a many gleaming rows and ridges of red, blue, and yellow. It darted its smooth beautiful head this way and that, when you folded your hand over its wings, and brought its head close to your face.

It died the following week. I found it on my desk one lunchtime. She had put it in a bamboo cage, and it sang all week, but one morning, she found it on the floor of the cage, covered in ants.

After that, we went to different secondary schools. I went to the local grammar that had opened down the beach, and she went someplace in Kumba.

But, she joined me in the local grammar, in the third year.

I recognised her on the first day after morning assembly. She stood in the middle of a group of admiring boys. A contingent of fifteen-year-old girls to her side looked on with suppressed envy. They looked, because even then, in their early learning curve, they knew that the glamour of the stars rubs off on their followers.

I approached the group to say, hey. After all, I had a greater claim to her than most, and she had murdered my bird four years back. She was bigger, fuller around the waist.

As I approached, one of the boys stuck out a toe. I tripped and fell against her bottom. She turned around and without hesitation, slapped me across the face. The groupies roared with laughter.

I thought to strike back, but she still had pretty eyes, so I said.

-Why did you do that? You and your fat bottom.

That was the most insult I could give.

-Hmm, she said, somebody, please tell this idiot that rich men like fat bottoms.

She waved her bottom at me, and the crowd cheered. I walked away, head on chest, and I did not speak to her again, until we both left school.

She did apologise years later for that perfect slap.

She had two teenage boys by then, and lived in a big house on the West Coast, to which the town of old Victoria had expanded and eventually claimed.

She was a good cook. After dinner, we sat on her veranda and looked over to the golden lights of the new oil refinery, gleaming yellow, on the surface of the Atlantic Ocean. So did she get the rich man she had always wanted?

-Yeah, she said.

She threw back her head and drained her wine.

-But be careful what you ask for. You just might get it. Excuse me.

She went into the house, and returned with another bottle of wine.

-So, do you now like fat arsed girls? She asked laughing.

-Tell me about your rich husband. Does he live here with you?

I had looked for man-signs in the living room with the glass-fronted cupboards, and red leather furniture. There was a white cage, where a silent green parrot stood on a stand at the far end near the window.

-We are not married. He has two wives, but he gave me two beautiful children. Sam and Ernestine. They are twins.

-Wow! So you've had a good life.

It was a statement, not a question. She laughed, and said.

-You remember your bird?

-What bird?

-The one you gave me.

-Ah, I do, the one, the one you killed.

-No, I think it died of boredom. I've kept parrots since, but they all die, so I keep getting new ones.

-Maybe birds don't want to be owned.

-Yes, even when the owner is wealthy.

-Wow. That's deep.

She filled my glass.

-I don't know what's so wow about it. You know the story of the woodpecker?

I did not.

The woodpecker boasted, that he will carve a coffin from a rock when his mum dies.

I still did not understand.

-Well, I met him when I was nineteen.

-That was early. I said.

I had a nineteen-year-old daughter by then, and I wouldn't let her marry at that age, if I can help it.

-He put me in this house, and I perfumed and waited for him, on the evenings he could make it.

-Did, did your mother really tell you all those things?

-What things?

-You know, the things about pretty girls.

-You remember shit, don't you? She died four years back. And your mother, is she still alive?

-No, she too, died five years ago. We're our own parents now.

-Sorry to hear that.

-Are you, were you happy? I ventured.

-Ah, happiness. You know, nobody gives it to you. Nobody can make you happy.

-Ha, that's not true, you know. My wife makes me happy.

-You believe that? You men believe shit.

-And women?

-Yes, us women, we know, we do not believe, that men like fat arsed girls.

I shook my head. Then she said again,

-Naa! You give yourself happiness; it's your job to make you happy.

She went quiet as if she had said too much. We sipped our red wine and stared at the lights glimmering on the calm ocean. Silence is golden, a friend once said, but so are the lights of the oil refinery in the night.

-When woodpecker's mother died, he had a boil on his beak, and he could not carve a wooden coffin, let alone a stone one.

-Haha.

-I had everything you know? Some jealous head once said, I was a caged bird.

-Absolute rubbish.

-But I tell you, now that his children need him most, he's gone plain broke, as broke as broke china.

-You don't' say? I said.

-Now, I don't know how I will send them to school.

-But, but, I stammered, you have this beautiful house.

-What house? Oh, this one? The bailiffs are coming tomorrow. It's his house.

Inside the house a telephone rang.

-Give me a second, will you?

She walked away from me, her arse swayed. When she joined me again on the veranda, she stared into the golden lights bordering the oil refinery, and at the refinery itself where a thin stream of black smoke rose into the air.

-It's too late now. They say, be careful of what you ask for, because you just might get it. Another glass?

She leaned to fill me up, and I looked down the front of her dress. I tilted my glass, and she filled it to the brim, with the red burning liquid.

THE LAZY EYE OF OLD DICKY CROW

Old Dicky Crow was a merry old soul. His family, friends, work colleagues, all agreed on this observation as the truth, the whole truth, and nothing but the truth. The regulars down at Mama Solange's in middle farms Bota, also made noises to the affirmative.

Mama Solange's was the place where he ate fried snails, and drank liberal quantities of cold beer, on any good day that the Lord hath made,

He was also a brilliant tenor, Old Dicky Crow, and gave the best rendition of, "take it to The Lord in Prayer, this side of the botanic gardens in the township of old Victoria.

His jokes were repeated over and over again. They were repeated on house verandas and beer houses, up and down this coastal town. But without the colour which only Old Dicky could bring to it. He was a good man, a good egg, and a good coconut, and if he had any glaring faults, they came in the form of a trinity.

The least important, which some would argue was only a display of good financial sense, was his tendency to stand a teacher's round at Mama Solange's.

A teacher's round was the habit of only standing beers for a few select. This had been perfected by members of the teaching profession in Victoria. These teachers' rounds, was contrary to the tradition of standing beers for everyone within sight distance, when your time came.

Not that Old Dicky Crow was particularly tight. He too, was not a hundred percent inoculated against the plague of alcohol induced generosity, which affected many a jolly good fellow in Victoria. It was just that, well, he made up for it with his jokes, and mellifluous singing.

The other fault, was his enduring bachelorhood. This was important in the eyes of his family, but not so important to his drinking friends. The reason for this was simple. If he were to marry, that fact, would deprive them of his company

Oftentimes, they teased him about it, and he rewarded them with his joke about the perils of pamperdom, which was the name he had given to the sacrament of holy matrimony. The third fault, which was not a fault because he could neither help nor conceal it, was his lazy eye. The left one.

The lazy eye disturbed friend and foe alike. His friends did not however, suffer from any misplaced notions of physical perfection. After all, his best mate Njoku had a clubfoot, his other mate Mbella had lost all of an entire eye, during an accident with a bee's nest up in the highlands of Wotutu when he was a boy.

His lazy eye disturbed them because, when old Dicky felt betrayed, deceived, or slighted, this eye, the left one, would fix the wrong doer, in a slow wobble. This could happen after unflattering laughter in the wake of one of his jokes, or when someone skipped him, during the dishing out of a round.

The whites would turn the colour of baby milk, and a look of unmerited hurt, would blaze out, and make the culprit uncomfortable for the whole evening.

But as he was a good fellow. If in the end you made good the slight by standing Old Dicky a beer, all was quickly forgotten.

Old Dicky was a bursar's clerk at the CDC oil palm plantation school, but this had no bearing on his tendency to give teacher's rounds, since he never taught in any classroom. But it had a direct impact on his decision to propose, and to be accepted in marriage, by a girl of nocturnal fame, a little less than half his age.

She was the first daughter of the night watchman, down at the CDC oil palm plantation warehouse. Some said her father's profession had something to do with her reputation.

But if old Dicky Crow's friends, had any worries of losing his much-cherished company after his taking of the holy sacrament of matrimony, their anxiety was soon put to one side. They observed, even though he kept shorter hours with them, there was a noticeable improvement in the quality of his jokes, and in his singing voice.

And what was more, Old Dicky started shunning the teachers round habit, and took to standing beers to all present at the time he announced a round.

This led Mola Mbella to declare, to Dicky's face, that he had the best singing voice in all Victoria. The next day, Mola Mbela extended this voice supremacy to all of central and west Africa, and ultimately, all of Africa. This was high honour indeed, as according to Mola Mbella, no other continent on God's won planet could touch his beloved continent, when it came to singing. So that made old Crow, the best singer in the entire universe. But those not gifted with Mola Mbella's eloquence, put it down, to the love of a good woman, in the person of his dear wife.

So the uproar, and outpour of grief was quite in order, when news filtered through one fine morning, that Old Dicky Crow was dead. Just like that.

He went home to his wife after a good evening at Mama Solange's, woke up in the morning as dead as a bowl of foo foo.

Witchcraft! Some shouted

Murder most foul, others chimed.

But nobody asked, why would anybody want to kill Old Dicky

Crow. Why would anybody want to deprive the section of Victoria town west of the botanic gardens, of his brilliant singing.

His best mates, Silvanus and Njoku, remembered his much-improved jokes. They remembered his much improved singing after his marriage, and they also remembered the young woman's reputation for nocturnal activities. This led them to conclude that he had died of too much enjoyment. Or too much excitement, and movement, which to Silvanus, husband of two, and father of eight and one on the way, were one and the same thing.

Old Dicky Crow was duly buried, but death-by-witchcraft stories circulated throughout the various sections of Victoria on the other side of the botanic gardens, and continued even after the post mortem report, made known that, he had died of a massive heart failure.

His young widow wallowed around in his house, not quite deciding what to do with herself. She did not have long to wait because, the news of Old Dicky's demise through too much shaking in bed replaced the stories that he had been killed by witchcraft. The bed shaking stories too spread. It spread beyond the boundaries of Victoria, and reached Sasse on the slope of the Mountain, a good twenty miles away.

She became a celebrity, just like Old Dicky, but this time, amongst old bored wives because she had hastened a man's end, by giving him, too much of a good thing. This was something which a good number of them wished they could. This news spread even beyond the peaks of mount Fako, and tumbled into Kumba on the other side of the mountain, right up to Kembong.

But young Perpetua, as that was how the young widow had been christened at birth, had a bigger worry.

This worry came from a picture on the wall in the living room of the house Old Dickie Crow had built. It was not the usual picture of the Christ with a bleeding heart. Neither was it one of a Christ saying quaint stuff like,

-I am the way, the light. and the truth.

No, it was a portrait of old Dicky Crow himself.

The photo had been taken at Batanwi studios at half mile, near the Agip petrol station, on the day old Dicky gathered enough courage to corner Perpetua's father, and put forward the marriage proposition.

It was a good picture, a good likeness of the dearly departed, but Perpetua claimed the one eye, the lazy one, followed her about the house, and launched accusatory winks at her person.

A meeting of both families could not resolve the problem, as taking down the picture, would have been sacrilege of the highest order. But when the young widow started reporting sightings of Old Dicky sleeping on the sofa, sightings of old Dicky walking about and singing, take it to the lord in prayer, especially when she was very engaged with a student from Sasse. After that, they agreed it was time to call in the local ghost buster.

This ghost hunter was no other than obassimjom, whose name means- the truth teller.

Obassimjom was no other than Ashu of Kembong, a strapping man of thirty-odd years. He formed a plan to find out for himself, if all he had heard, was as it was.

Ashu presented himself to the family as the spokesperson for the caster of demons. He listened, took one look at Perpetua, and decided that she needed a week's stay in his house for spiritual cleansing.

Perpetua was not warm to this idea, as she was a middle farms girl through and through, and to add insult to injury, Ashu lived in Kembong, which was in a land, far far away.

All seemed at a standstill until Ashu decided he could not forgo the fee coming the way of the obassimjom. He fixed a day for obassimjom to get rid of the singing Dicky, whom the good lord had already called to do same in the great big choir up in the sky.

The day came and Obassimjom did not show. The families checked up on Ashu, to explain this lamentable failure to keep to an arrangement.

They found Ashu dead from a sudden heart attack in his bed. But whether this had anything to do with Perpetua or not, is still hotly debated by the good people of old Victoria.

But all was not lost. Old Dicky's friends began to miss their mate to such an extent that, they held an emergency session to decide what to do about all this missing.

The meeting held at Mama Solange's, with Mola Mbela as the nominated chair. After a quick observance of the necessary protocols, the moved to item nine on the agenda, which was an airing by the members present, of what they missed most about Old Dicky crow.

Of course they mentioned his singing, his jokes, his abandon of the teacher's round.

-Anything else? Mola Mbella asked.

He let the silence dwell for a few seconds, and then he answered his own question.

-I miss his lazy eye.

The friends gathered considered the statement for a minute and a half. They sipped their beers with moist eyes, and sighed repeatedly. But it was Njoku who came up with the suggestion that would put an end to all that misty eyeing.

Why don't we ask Perpetua, if we could transfer the picture here, that way, we would not only hear him singing, but see his lazy eye do its thing.

-But that would be going against tradition!

They nodded. Yes, it would be going against tradition. But Njoku would not be easily dissuaded.

-We all know this place was a second home to our dearly departed friend, Dicky.

He stood up, like he always did when he felt he was onto a good thing.

-We could explain to the family; we are only taking him, to his second home.

THE BENEFITS
OF HOUSE FIRE
INSURANCE

I used to hustle down at the Atlantic Beach Hotel Victoria, shepherding tourists to the zoo, the crater lake, and mile six beach, for a small fee. I did it seven days a week. But that was not my main source of income. My money came from burning houses. My official job as a shepherd did not pay much, but served a purpose. It provided a neutral place to find me, those who needed some burning. It was bad security if everybody knew where a professional house burner lived.

Back in the day, eighty percent of the houses in Victoria were made of wood, and thatch. They were easy to burn, and a lot of people did the easier thing, and asked others to do it for them. They asked me.

My clients were mostly people looking to settle a grievance, not like the clients we have nowadays, who are only interested in the insurance money. I know, some people might find this hard to believe, but if you hear a house or a car is on fire, do very well to check whether it has been insured.

When the old man found out what I did officially, he said that was not a job for a man, and his family totem did not allow for servant work. I wondered what he would have said, if he knew what I really did?

Our family totem was the Njoku, the elephant. Elephants do not act as guide dogs, he said. I followed his advice and gave up the official job, and took up an apprenticeship in a carpentry workshop in Lumpsum quarters.

People looking to burn down houses still knew where to find me, but the workshop gave me an edge over my competitors.

I learnt more about wood, the hardness, and most importantly how the hardness affected the time it took for a house to burn down, how much kerosene and petrol to use, did you need flaming gum? Those technicalities were lost on the amateurs. I bet you, every time you hear of a house that did not burn down completely, know that it was the work of an amateur.

Business boomed. With the boom, I could now go up to the village and show off during funerals, a gift of a pig here, a jug of palm wine there. The old man wanted me to join the elephant cult, but I held him off.

-But you have enough to pay for the initiation.

The initiation did cost a bit, what with all the food and alcohol one had to buy. But I did not want to join.

There was a rumour that if you had a bad heart, did bad things, the elephants would turn on you. Mola Vakise, who was an armed robber down in Douala, died a year after his initiation. He was trampled by elephants during a hunting trip; so you can understand my unwillingness

But I attended funerals, and bought food and drink. My father made sure I knew of every funeral. He kept inviting me, as a respectable citizen, to funerals for people I knew, those of whom I know little, and people I did not know who had died in far-flung places like Buea, Tiko and Douala.

I do not know whether he really believed an apprentice carpenter made all that money, but I understood his desire to remind the villagers that he has an inheritor for when he dies, and a strong male one, for that matter.

But I soon tired of funerals. Recently, we have had so many deaths that if I went up to the village every time, I would never complete my apprenticeship. My master, Mola Peter, the carpenter in Lump Sum quarters, even told my father so.

But the last letter said Auntie Sophie died. This one was my uncle's wife. I had to go.

My Uncle Mola Lisonge is known for his fiery temper. He is the head of the elephant cult, and some gossiped he was the only member of the group, who honestly had the elephant spirit in him, the Njoku. I do not know how true the rumour, but I know if he got going on you, God and his mother Mary help you.

But that was not why I had to obey the call in the letter. My uncle's wife was my mother. She was my wet nurse when my own mother died in the pain of bringing me into the village. I wake up before sunrise to make the trip. It was a Friday.

The tractor was the only way up, and it was common knowledge they picked up passengers for a small extra something. You could use the VW the priests use, but you needed to be a good catholic, otherwise getting on it was as unlikely an occurrence as an elephant that does not trample on cocoyam farms.

I had my old man's letters in the back pocket, as I walk up from Lump Sum, through the short-cut in cassava farms, to animal farms, then the road from animal farms, through the comprehensive college. From there, it was about a mile up the old road past the water treatment plant, to the Wototu Junction to wait for tractor drivers moving palm fruits from plantations to oil mills in Bota and Moliwe.

The ones going to my village came down from Moliwe. They passed through Bonadikombo, and then head up to Wototu, and just before Bojongo, they branched down to Karata.

The trick was as follows; when the tractor stopped, passengers jump off, and you climb onto an empty seat. The driver usually looks behind to check the empty spaces, but he can never keep count. He will be thinking, did three, or four get off; is that guy, a plantation worker and so entitled to a free ride?

I am third time unlucky slipping past the driver. Fourth time maybe? The blue light of the dawn is almost here. I cross my fingers and wait for the next tractor.

My fourth one makes its way through the crowd of early hawkers with their groundnuts, bananas and bread. It is packed. A few of the guys on the tractor buy bread. I brace myself. I could walk the distance in less than an hour, pay for the ride, but I liked seeing the look on the driver's face when he is not sure what happened? How many got off?

But before I could join the leaping passengers, this old man jumps off with a young man about my age.

His jacket catches my eye. It was one of those black pin-striped things. He wore a Cameroon airlines T-shirt underneath the jacket, and oversized khaki shorts with a skull cap lined with cowries. The young man, wears an identical hat and looks like a man going to a funeral up in the grasslands.

One of the guys on the back of the tractor throws down a raffia bag. It is red, yellow and green like the ones, you get from the Presbyterian arts and crafts centre. It had beautiful yellow tassels hanging down the sides. They look left and right, new chickens in the yard. My former hustling instincts stir in my head.

No, I am not thinking of nicking their bag or anything, but I have this feeling, something will come out of these two, but whether this something will be good or bad, I do not know. The veins at the side of my eyes start twitching.

I forget about the tractor, and follow them through the maze of taxis picking up passengers by the road to Mutengene. They two stop in front of a woman selling boiled maize and plums. I could at least get one off them. I make my move. After all, I have hustled

German, French and Italian tourists at the Atlantic Beach Hotel. These two would be easy.

-Hmm, I cough. Do you want to go somewhere?

They look at me, and then the young man looks at the old man.

-I can help you get a clean taxi for three hundred francs.

The old man gives me this yellow stare from beneath bushy brows. My knees go weak. I swear, I must have been standing there for about two years. Then he says,

-My son, we're going to Wvojongo.

He pronounces my village's name the way a real Bojongo man would pronounce it.

He wanted to know if I could point them in the right direction, and he would be most grateful. I do not tell him, if he had stayed on the tractor, he would have been in Bojongo ten minutes ago.

-We could walk, I venture, and I'll escort you there for five hundred francs.

The old man gives me his bag. It is too heavy for five hundred francs, but I make no complaint. I indicate the direction and we start to walk in silence. Questions race in my mind but, every time I turn to ask, the old man is too far behind me. We walk up in a file.

They want to see our chief, and my heart skips a beat, because my father had mentioned the chief on some troublesome matter between the chief and my uncle.

When we got to the village, I receive my five hundred francs and point out the chief's house.

The old man is happy to see me.

-But you're late. The burial was yesterday.

I think to show him his letter where it said the burial is tomorrow, but think better of it.

-But I'm glad you came. There's a meeting at the chief's this evening, and I'll like you to accompany me. You're no longer a boy you know.

-What's it about?

-Our people are dying.

He did not need to say much. We had lost three members of our family in the last week.

When we get to the chief's palace, the village old men had formed a circle around the old man from the tractor. I whisper to my father.

-I brought that man to the village today.

He says to shush. The old man from the tractor lights a candle and places it on the floor. He opens the bag I had carried and pours out the contents. Cowries and blackened monkey paws and bits of string fall out.

We all inch in closer.

We watch. Something is happening. One of the red strings stands upright like a cobra, and starts to talk. I glance at the medicine man. He is frantically chewing on something. He spit-aims at the string. Every time he spits, the rope dodges the stream of black saliva, and says something. The old man says something back, which I could only decipher as hmm.

The young man with the gourd sits cross-legged just outside the circle of old men and beats two sticks together.

-There is evil in the land. The old man says. The young man beats his sticks, hmm, spit, dodge.

-People are dying.

We know all that! I think to myself. I hope he did not come to the village to tell us what my father's letters tell me every week.

-The evil came on a tractor from Victoria, and now lives in a house under two orange trees. Look for those orange trees.

We walk back in silence, and stop by my uncle's to pay my respects. When we get to the two orange trees in front of his house, he sits on the bamboo bench under one of the trees. Up in my uncle's house, there is the glow of his hurricane lamp. I too sit.

-My son, you've seen what you've seen today. You've heard what you've heard. There is so much evil. Be careful.

I stay quiet because I do not know where this talk of evil is going. I ask

-Did you believe that medicine man?

-Who else was on the tractor today?

I feel alarmed. He senses my fear, and says,

-No need for that, let's go in and meet my brother.

-Father, I say. The orange trees. The medicine man said two orange trees.

-Not now, there are many orange trees in the village.

I point to the orange trees in front of my uncle's house.

-What? Oh, my brother is no evil. He has a temper, and that's all. He's like our father.

He gets up, and I follow him into the house.

My uncle slaps me around the head when he sees me.

-Is it now you come?

-Don't hit the boy, my father says.

-So, I shouldn't hit him. He's your son now? Is this how it is now?

I look about the house, the tell-tale signs of a recent funeral, chairs, beer bottles.

-Come, you will see the grave in the morning, we buried your mother under the soursop tree.

My father and uncle have always been close, and they have always fought and it was worse when they were boys. But uncle has no child of his own, and as far back as I can remember, I am his son.

-Father, you know with all the work, the letters always arrive too late.

-So why did you go to the chief? Uncle asks.

I had not noticed he was not at the talking string meeting.

-One of us had to be there, to know what they're on about.

-You know what? This's all about a bit of land. The chief says I shouldn't have sold it. Then, he sold my land near our plantain farm on the road to Wotutu, to a policeman.

Father coughs. I watch his face. The lamp wick dances in his eyes. I know he and his elder brother had some words about some land their father left. But this is not the time for such talk. We just lost a mother.

-The chief says people are dying, and he's brought this medicine man.

-Rubbish, I tell you, he's looking for trouble, and there will be trouble in this village.

-Nothing will happen. We've had medicine men come in the past about this Nyongo thing.

But there is a harried look on my father's face. I wonder whether he's thinking of the two orange trees in front of my uncle's house. They've been there as far back as I can remember, it has been there so long, I cannot count the number of times I have sold oranges from these trees in Wototu market.

Later, at about two or three in the morning, I open my eyes. There is a noise of women and children screaming as if somebody has died during the night. I tie a cloth around my loin, and my father takes down his machetes and gives me the big one. We approach the centre of the noise. My uncle's house under the two orange trees was in flames.

-Follow me, Father says.

We take the path behind our house to the grove where our family keeps the shrine, and find uncle cowering inside the hut.

-Who's it? He shouts at our footsteps on dry leaves.

-It's me.

I wonder whether uncle was afraid. You see, the only place nobody would dare follow anyone unless they are of the same blood, is the family shrine.

-I told you, the chief wants my head.

-What do we do?

-Follow me, I say.

There was something about seeing my uncle's house on fire, that disturbed me. You could tell who ever did it was an amateur. They did not use any gum. I will show them how it is done.

-Follow you?

-Did you not say I am no longer a boy?

We take the back paths and arrive at the chief's house. My father and uncle hide in the darkness, I knock on the door and inquire if the medicine man is in the house. Somebody tells me he is staying with the chief's uncle further down the village.

We go down the village to look for the medicine mam, but there is nobody at there. We stand in front of the house for some time.

-Wait for me here. I say, just in case the medicine comes back.

-What are you going to do?

-I need petrol, and the paste of a gum tree.

-Are you mad? I father says.

-Shut up, leave the boy alone! My uncle shouts to his brother.

-Wait for me here.

My father does not argue with him whenever he starts talking really fast. Nobody does. The rushing speech means the Njoku spirit has descended on him.

I disappear and get to work. I leave the chief's house for later. We had to do this as a family. When I come back, my uncle pats me on the back.

-More than one house is on fire today.

-Yes uncle.

-We should've done this a long time ago. My uncle says

I wave my Machete for them to follow.

-Where are we going? My father asks.

-To the chief's house again.

The chief's dog barks at us, and I bring it down with the machete. Uncle climbs onto the veranda and starts pouring out the rest of the fuel. I fix the gum.

When we got home, Father brings out some palm wine. He proposes a toast to the ancestors.

-I'm sorry about your house, but you can always come and stay with me.

Uncle laughs. He laughs so hard I begin to worry the funeral and the house fires had gone into his brain. Fire does that sometime. I have seen people whose houses I had burnt, walking around Victoria talking to themselves.

-Excuse me, He says. It is just that, the chief refused to buy insurance for his house the other week, when Mola Esunge's son came here. The one who works for the insurance company.

-And?

-And, I did!

EPILOGUE

BOOKS BY THIS AUTHOR

The Smell Of Yellow

Some of the stories in this collection have been short listed in various International Short Story Competitions. Guilt received an Honorary mention in the Lorian Hemingway Short Story competition back in 2006. I am presenting them here for the first time.
Its geographic spread is a metaphor for the universality of the human condition. It looks at the kaleidoscope of what it means to be human and weak. But it also touches on love and hope without which all the other things that make us human would be impossible.

However in the end the reader is free to draw out whatever they find in them

The Victoria Chronicles Volume 1

This collection of short stories is set in and around the town of old victoria located on the Man O' War bay coast to the west of the Rio del Rey.
The government changed the name of the town to Limbe, but to some it still remains Victoria from of a sense of nostalgia. The stories drip with this nostalgia and reflect the passing of time from innocence to whatever happens after innocence.
It is still a boisterous beautiful town and the stories in this volume would be familiar to anybody who grew up in Victoria. Those not so fortunate will derive some pleasure from reading

them.

History says in 1858 Alfred Saker founded the first European settlements in Victoria but failed to convince the English government to make the area a crown colony.

Just as well, the English returned after the Germans lost in the Great War, and war did something similar to what Alfred Saker failed to do in 1858.

The Three Wise Men, St Peter The Jedi And Other Yarns

This collection of short stories is set in the Middle East in and around the year 1BC, and told with echoes of time travel between the then, and the now. Various characters tell them, followers of Jesus, casual unnamed observers, and in one case one of the Wise men of Christmas Carol fame.

They stories come in a humorous exaggerated way, flipping through time to create an accessible narrative, told the way the man on the streets, the children down at the estates, the wide boys, the wannabe cool kids would have told and probably understood them.

There are nine stories in this collection covering the miracle at Cana, the Three Wise Men, the Holy Spirit descending on the apostles and other totemic happenings of those times.

How To Be An Excellent Student: The Student's Guide

This book is your guide to awesomeness.

It guides, teaches on how to study and acquire know-how that becomes inseparable from your person, knowledge that defines who you are as a student, an employee, and an individual.

It is a guide to all who study whether they seek academic qualifications or otherwise. It is for those who seek only mastery and perfect understanding of that which they set their minds to internalise.

Comment Devenir Un Étudiant Exceptionnel: Le Guide De L'étudiant (French Edition)

L'objectif de ce livre est simple : vous montrer comment devenir un(e) étudiant(e) exceptionnel(le). Les outils qu'il vous donnera sont simples à maitriser ; son langage est simple. Ce livre vous guide et vous enseigne les méthodes à utiliser pour étudier et acquérir des connaissances qui deviendront inséparables, indissociables de votre personnalité toute votre vie

Limbe (known as Victoria from 1858 to 1982) is a seaside city in the South-West Region of Cameroon. At the 2005 Census, the population was 84,223.Untitled